CAPTIVE HEARTS

Listen for the Call

To Avis

Thessa Chamberlain

Romans 10:13-15

12/6/03

CAPTIVE
HEARTS

Listen for the Call

THRESA CHAMBERLAIN

Pleasant Word
A Division of WINEPRESS PUBLISHING

Packaged by Pleasant Word, a division of WinePress Publishing, PO Box 428, Enumclaw, WA 98022. The views expressed or implied in this work do not necessarily reflect those of Pleasant Word. The author(s) is ultimately responsible for the design, content and editorial accuracy of this work.

All scripture references are taken from the King James Version of the Bible.

ISBN 1-4141-0001-9
Library of Congress Catalog Card Number: 2003107677

Dedication

This book is dedicated to all my family members who encouraged me to write—especially my husband Steve, my children Tonya, Travis and Seth, and my mother Lois.

Thank you for your prayers and support.

Table of Contents

Historical Note

The town of Julesburg acquired its name from the infamous Jules Beni, an agent for the Overland Stage Company who ran a trading post on the south side of the Platte River during the 1850s. The town of Julesburg moved three times before it reached its fourth and final destination.

Julesburg #1 was the only Pony Express station in Colorado. It was designated as a "home station," where both horse and rider were switched. Indians burned the first Julesburg in February 1865. Much of the South Platte River Trail between "Devil's Dive" and Julesburg #1 was stained with blood during the great Indian raids of early 1865. The "Dive" is a deep, rugged wash of rock, cactus, sand and sagebrush that earned its name from stagecoach drivers. Many travelers described it as possibly the most dangerous part of the old trail route.

The second Julesburg was established in 1866. This town served primarily as a stage station, but it was abandoned in 1867.

Julesburg moved to its third location when the Union Pacific Railroad reached the "End of Tracks" north of the river. Because of its numerous saloons and gambling houses, Julesburg #3 earned its title as the "wickedest city in the West."

When the Union Pacific constructed a Denver branch line in 1881, a new town was founded at the rail junction. Most of the population soon abandoned the third Julesburg in favor of this new town of Denver Junction. However, the popularity of Jules Beni's legacy prevailed and Denver Junction was soon renamed Julesburg at its fourth and final location.

This historical information was obtained from the information center at Julesburg, Colorado.

Chapter One

Elizabeth stood rooted to the ground, her eyes fixed on the warrior. He stood tall and proud, watching the horses thunder around her in circles as men reached toward her with clubs and spears. The rawhide thongs that bound her wrists in front of her were so tight they burned. She watched as the hot summer wind rippled her skirt around her ankles.

Elizabeth wavered slightly as the spear point creased her shoulder and ripped her sleeve. Praying silently, she held her eyes steady with those of the tall warrior. If this was to be the end, she prayed God would allow her to die quickly. She would not cry out or beg for her life. Elizabeth Mayfield would not give these savages the satisfaction of her screams.

When the blood trickled down her arm, it reached her bound wrists and dripped to the ground. Elizabeth knew the wound was deep, but why worry. She would most likely be dead by nightfall.

Although the tall warrior was young, Elizabeth decided he must be the chief. He lifted his hand and motioned to the circling riders. The screams and yips of the warriors stopped as they lined up their horses to face him. Silence hung heavily in the air. Elizabeth thought she saw a faint glimmer in the chief's eye, and then ever so slightly a smile played at his lips.

Elizabeth was mortified that these people could enjoy torturing other humans. "Savages, that's what they are," she remembered her father telling her when she was a little girl. At the time she thought he was cold and heartless to say such a thing. But now she knew her father had been right.

Daniel Mayfield had begged his strong-willed daughter to stay in the East. But at age twenty-two Elizabeth could not stay put any longer. She had answered an ad in the *Chicago Tribune* for a live-in housekeeper for an elderly couple in Denver. Elizabeth had started west a week later. The long train ride seemed unbearable—until she had been on the stage a few days. She was beginning to think she wouldn't make it in the West, not if she couldn't even endure a stage ride.

The Cheyenne had descended on the stagecoach quickly and killed the shotgun guard and the driver. Two men, the only other passengers aboard the stage, fought fiercely in an effort to protect Elizabeth. But the Indians killed them and Elizabeth was taken captive. The warriors roughly bound her wrists.

After tossing her among themselves, the Indian with the bald head and small beady eyes threw her astride his paint pony. As they raced toward the hills, she felt weak and dizzy. Her father's words rang in her ears, throbbing with each beat of the horses' pounding hooves: "savages . . . savages . . . savages."

The Cheyenne raiding party traveled the rest of that day and all night, stopping only once to let the horses and men drink at a stream. Elizabeth managed to get a small portion of water to her mouth, but the rawhide thongs that bound her wrists were painfully tight.

The small group reached the Cheyenne village at mid-morning. Children of all ages shouted and played as they ran alongside the horses. Forgetting their daily activities, the people of the village were drawn by the commotion. The riders stopped at the door of a large tepee. Villagers came around the group to see the white woman that the raiding party had brought in. The ugly, bald Indian shoved Elizabeth from the pony's back and laughed as she hit the sun-baked earth.

The three ruthless warriors circled around her as Elizabeth stumbled to her feet. When she reached her full height she set her jaw determinedly and stared into the eyes of the tall warrior that had emerged from the tepee. Elizabeth found the strange screams and chants of the warriors unnerving as they raced around her. She steadied herself as the bald Indian with the beady eyes, sliced her shoulder with his spear. She would die here in the hands of these savages, but she prayed God would give her strength. The words of Isaiah 41:10 went through her mind: *Fear thou not; for I am with thee: be not dismayed; for I am thy God: I will strengthen thee; yea, I will help thee.*

The tall, proud Indian spoke loudly and with authority-first in English and then in his own language, "The white woman will not die." Elizabeth wished for death; it would be better to die than to be at the mercy of these savages. "The white woman will not die," he repeated with final authority.

The big Indian wearing eagle claws around his neck, jerked his horse cruelly around making it pranced wildly as the angry retort from his master reached The tall, proud Indian. "She must die; she is a white dog."

"Not all whites are bad," The tall Indian replied sternly. "This one lives; she is brave!"

The big Indian wearing eagle claws glared at the chief. Then swinging his horse around quickly, he spat on Elizabeth and rode away in a fury.

Elizabeth was stunned. Her instincts to live were pulling at her heart with hope, but reality was clouding that hope. She had been prepared to die. She knew where she would go when she died. She was a born-again child of God. Death did not frighten her, only the method of death.

The crowd parted as the chief moved through it, pulling his knife from the beaded sheath that hung at his hip. Elizabeth saw the sun glint on the blade as he came near her. She extended her wrists toward the chief boldly, lifting her eyes to his as he reached her. Their eyes held momentarily before he slashed the pieces of rawhide from her wrists.

Elizabeth worked her fingers and rubbed her wrists to get the circulation back in her hands. With that effort also came a throbbing pain that reminded her that her shoulder needed tending.

She looked around in amazement as the village people wandered back to their lodges as though they had been out for a Sunday afternoon stroll. Women returned to their work, children to their play and warriors to various activities. The tall chief was nowhere in sight. It was as though she had been forgotten in a matter of minutes.

Elizabeth stood still briefly, wondering what she should do. Was she free to go or was she being watched? Slowly Elizabeth walked toward the stream. She reached the water and still no one seemed to notice her. Ripping a piece of white cotton from her petticoat, she dipped it into the chilly waters. She needed hot water but for now this would have to do. Cleansing the wound carefully, Elizabeth then ripped more strips of cloth and bandaged her shoulder tightly, hoping it would heal properly.

Several squaws and young girls came to the stream to dip water. Elizabeth spoke to each one, hoping to get at least a friendly gesture in return. But each one acted the same, ignoring her as if she weren't there. They didn't even look her way.

Elizabeth felt so very alone. What would she do now? She sat at the water's edge in deep thought for many hours. Pulling her legs up under her she suddenly realized she was shivering. The nights were cold in the mountains and she had only a thin cotton dress.

As her thoughts raced on, she sensed she was not alone. Elizabeth had not heard a sound, yet there stood the chief.

He handed Elizabeth a large buffalo robe saying. "The night will be cold."

"Thank you," replied Elizabeth as she took the robe.

"I am Standing Arrow," he said pointing to himself. "And what are you called?"

"Elizabeth . . . where did you learn to speak English?"

Squatting down beside her he said solemnly, "White man comes to our village. We are friends. We hunt together." With a look of bewilderment, Standing Arrow asked "Why you sit here on bank and shake? You are free. You should be half day walk from camp."

Elizabeth knew this was true. Smiling thoughtfully she replied, "Yes, but I don't know the forest, and I know if I leave here those warriors that captured me would most likely kill me."

"You are right," answered Standing Arrow. "Black Crow and his men cause me much grief. The big one's name is Eagle Claw and the one with no hair is Snake. Black Crow is the third one. He is the chief of the Dog Soldiers," explained Standing Arrow. "Maybe I keep you for my friend, Trent," he said thoughtfully. "He need wife."

Elizabeth, her mouth agape, turned quickly to look at him.

"Maybe you rather Snake or Black Crow," he said with amusement in his voice.

Elizabeth giggled out loud saying, "No, thank you."

For the first time she saw a broad smile on the chief's face and a twinkle in his dark eyes. "Trent lives in the mountains and traps beavers. He will be coming soon."

16

A flame of hope leaped in Elizabeth's heart. If he came he would surely return her to the closest white settlement.

Standing Arrow was speaking as she returned from her thoughts. "Come to my lodge. My mother will be happy to share her work and tend to your wound. She is called is Little Robin."

Elizabeth, unsure if she wanted to go to his lodge, got to her feet holding the buffalo robe tightly about her. It was cumbersome and smelled of bear fat but she was thankful for the warmth. The crisp and clear air smelled good to Elizabeth.

It was a short walk that brought them to the center of camp where the largest tepee loomed in the darkness, casting shadows across the moonlit camp.

As Elizabeth entered the tepee, warm air and a crackling fire greeted her. She felt almost at ease and could have forgotten she was a long way from civilization and in the middle of a Cheyenne camp. As her eyes met the cold black eyes of Standing Arrows mother, she knew she was not welcome.

Standing Arrow, unconcerned at his mother's behavior, instructed her in their language to care for Elizabeth's shoulder and explained that when it was better Elizabeth would in return help with the work. Elizabeth didn't know what Little Robin's reply was but knew by the angry retort that she needed no help from Elizabeth. Little Robin reached for a small deerskin bag that was adorned with colorful designs.

Standing Arrow motioned for Elizabeth to sit in front of Little Robin. Reluctantly Elizabeth obeyed. Little Robin placed dried leaves in a hollowed-out spot in a rock and began grinding them to make a poultice. Fascinated, Elizabeth watched while Little Robin prepared the medicine. All too soon Little Robin was roughly unwinding the bloody strips from Elizabeth's shoulder and applying the poultice of dry leaves to the wound.

Despite the unkind treatment from Little Robin, Elizabeth was feeling better. Soft strips of buckskin were then placed over the injury and wrapped tightly. Little Robin spoke short harsh words repeatedly while pointing to a large buffalo hide on the floor. Even though the words were unfamiliar to her, Elizabeth knew Little Robin was trying to tell her that was where she was to sleep.

Exhausted, Elizabeth dropped onto the robe, her mind whirling over the day's events, wondering what she would do now. There was no hope of rescue. Even she knew she should be dead. The stage line would have found the others and most likely would assume she was taken by the Indians, tortured and killed a slow unmerciful death. No one in their right mind went out in these vast mountains and canyons to an Indian camp to search for captives. Her only thread of hope was the white man Standing Arrow had spoken of, but how soon would it be until he showed up?

Lord, Elizabeth prayed, *You've spared me this far for reasons unknown. Please give me strength to endure the days ahead and help me know what to do. I need You, Lord. I'm scared. I know Your Word says You will never leave me or for-sake me.* With renewed peace, she drifted off to sleep.

Chapter Two

As the sun peeked over the horizon, the Cheyenne camp came alive. Fires were started and the sounds of activity resumed. Elizabeth got to her feet, an unconscious moan slowly escaping her mouth as she remembered where she was. She looked around the tepee, hoping Little Robin or Standing Arrow hadn't heard her.

Every muscle in her body screamed painfully as she moved, especially as she slowly stooped down to fit through the door of the lodge. Elizabeth went directly to the stream and used her good hand to scoop the water to her mouth for a refreshing drink. Then she washed her face. It was difficult to do a good job using only one hand, but movement in her right shoulder was more than she could bear this morning. Fiery pain shot through her arm with every beat of her heart.

Elizabeth knew the wrap was too tight and was causing the circulation to be cut off in her arm. But could she manage to get the bandage off without help? Little Robin would most likely refuse, so asking her was out of the question. The knot that held the strips in place was very tight and in a difficult spot for her to reach. Elizabeth worked carefully, pulling only as hard as the pain would allow.

If only she had a knife, she could have cut right through the knot, cleaned the wound and replaced the bandage by now. Frustration broke into anger and anger into tears, which she quickly wiped away. She could not allow anyone to see her cry. She must maintain her composure at all times; that would be her only chance of survival.

The words of Philippians 4:13 raced through her mind: *I can do all things through Christ which strengtheneth me.*

Unable to remove the bandage, Elizabeth decided to walk through the camp. Maybe Standing Arrow was back. By the time Elizabeth had awakened, he was already gone from the close confines of camp, leaving her at Little Robin's mercy. Little Robin had not offered her anything to eat or drink. Her last meal had been breakfast two days ago at the stage stop. Although she knew she needed nourishment, Elizabeth didn't really feel like eating.

As she threaded her way slowly through camp, she observed the women as they worked on various things. Scraping hides didn't hold her interest long. It looked to be a long, laborious chore. *How do they make them so soft?* she wondered. *Why aren't any of the men helping?* She didn't understand why the men were all sitting around talking or sleeping in the sun while the women were laboring so hard.

Elizabeth walked past large strips of meat drying on racks. She watched squaws grinding berries, children playing and groups of warriors talking around the fire. No one spoke or even looked at her. She was amazed that even the young children didn't stare or look her way.

After searching all through camp, Elizabeth did not find Standing Arrow. Slowly she headed back to the stream. As she rounded the last of the tepees, she spotted Standing Arrow. He was talking with two warriors. Elizabeth hung back, waiting for him to end his conversation before approaching him. To her surprise he turned and headed off through camp.

"Standing Arrow," Elizabeth called out. As she quickened her pace, Standing Arrow walked steadily on. She knew he had heard her. Why didn't he stop?

Bewildered, she stood there and watched him until he reached the other side of camp. Confusion and hurt filled her mind. Why would Standing Arrow be kind last night and ignore her today? She turned slowly toward the stream and walked dejectedly to the water's edge.

As Elizabeth dipped cool water from the stream and lifted it to her lips, she realized how thirsty she was. But it hadn't been that long ago since she had had a drink. Surely she shouldn't be that thirsty. She drank deeply and settled back to rest before resuming her task of removing the bandage. After a few feeble attempts she had made no progress. Elizabeth took a few minutes and prayed that God would help her, give her strength and continue to watch over her. She remembered what it said in Matthew

21:22: "*And all things, whatsoever ye shall ask in prayer, believing, ye shall receive.*"

 With new determination Elizabeth set to work untying the knot. She had to get it loosened soon or the swelling would continue to make matters worse. Elizabeth was beginning to feel dizzy and beads of perspiration were forming on her forehead. When she finally got the knot loose, she unwound the strips carefully. But she was not prepared for the pain that followed as the blood rushed unrestrained through her veins. Nausea and dizziness overcame her, leaving her slumped in a heap at the edge of the stream.

⎯⎯⎯◦⎯⎯⎯

When Standing Arrow had turned to leave, he had heard the white woman call out to him. But he had walked steadily away from her without hesitating even momentarily. He had heard the pleading in her voice as she had come closer only to be left standing alone. Still Standing Arrow had walked on. He was thankful she hadn't persisted. It would have only made it harder on her. It was not an easy task to earn respect.

⎯⎯⎯◦⎯⎯⎯

As Elizabeth lay unconscious, her fever rose dangerously high. She regained consciousness only to find that she was drenched in sweat. Shakily, she crawled into the water and submerged her entire body. The cool water felt refreshing.

As Elizabeth stumbled out of the water, trying to hold her dress up with one hand, she began to shiver slightly. That was good, the fever had broken, at least for awhile. Before she could finish drip-drying, the slight shivers had turned to violent shaking. Elizabeth made her way back to the lodge and crawled under the heavy buffalo robe, wrapping it tightly about her. She tried to pray and then fell into a fitful sleep.

Little Robin entered the tepee, grumbling that the white woman was not working and was sleeping in the middle of the day. When Standing Arrow came back, she would tell him about the lazy white woman, and then she would be made to work or die. Little Robin continued her work outside the tepee until supper was ready.

As Standing Arrow made his way to the fire for supper, Little Robin told him that the white woman was lazy and had slept all day. "She doesn't deserve to eat," Little Robin concluded.

Silently, Standing Arrow ate the food his mother had prepared and listened to her condemn the white woman. *How odd,* Standing Arrow thought, *that she would sleep most of the day.* Looking at his mother he ask "Did you feed her and care for her wound?"

Little Robin turned her back to him and busied herself.

"Did you?" Standing Arrow asked firmly.

"No," retorted Little Robin angrily.

Entering the lodge, Standing Arrow knelt beside the buffalo robe and began pulling it off of Elizabeth. He was alarmed when he heard a moan escape her lips as he moved about her. As the last layer was pulled back, Standing Arrow's pulse quickened at the sight of Elizabeth. Her long blonde hair had fallen down from the tight knot she had had it pinned in. It lay tangled and damp in clumps around her shoulders.

As he touched her brow, Standing Arrow jumped up quickly. The fever was raging. She must be cared for or she would die.

In three long strides, Standing Arrow was at Little Robin's side. Ordering her to get cool water from the stream, he went back inside the lodge, knelt beside Elizabeth and covered her, leaving her wounded shoulder exposed.

He removed the crude bandage Elizabeth had tried to replace after crawling out of the stream. What an ugly sight! He had not realized it was that bad. The spear had torn a jagged path to the bone and left a gaping wound on the back side of her arm. It was swollen and red with infection.

Returning to the fire, Standing Arrow dipped warm liquid from the venison stew into a hollowed-out gourd that served as a bowl. Kneeling beside Elizabeth, he lifted her head carefully, putting the bowl to her lips. Standing Arrow patiently let the life-giving fluid run into her mouth and down her throat.

When he was satisfied that Elizabeth had drunk enough, Standing Arrow went to look for his mother. She was slowly carrying a small amount of water from the stream. As she reached the lodge, Little Robin saw Standing Arrow in front of the tepee. He had an angry frown across his face.

She concluded that although he was her son, he was also the chief and it would be wise to obey him, so she picked up her pace. In time he would see that the white woman was only a burden.

While Little Robin bathed Elizabeth's face in the cool water, Standing Arrow went across camp to the medicine man's lodge. "You are needed at my lodge," instructed Standing Arrow.

He then proceeded to Nakoma's lodge. Drawing near, Standing Arrow hailed his friend. Nakoma pulled back the tepee door, allowing Standing Arrow to enter. "Nakoma," said Standing Arrow, "the white woman is hot with fever, will Yellow Flower come and care for her?"

Nakoma's brow furrowed as he looked at Standing Arrow. "What can Yellow Flower do that Little Robin cannot?" asked Nakoma.

"Yellow Flower will care for her because she does not like death. Little Robin will care for her only because I force her to. And when I am not there she does not care for her. It will do Little Robin good to have Yellow Flower come to my lodge and do Little Robin's duty."

Nakoma nodded to Yellow Flower. She eagerly gathered her herb pouch and hastily followed Standing Arrow.

Little Robin had returned to the stream, dipping a larger amount of water in a short amount of time. She continued to bathe Elizabeth's face and neck. It would be a long process and lots of trips to the stream for cool water. *Maybe she will die soon* thought Little Robin.

Looking up, she saw Standing Arrow come through the door with Yellow Flower behind him. Angrily Little Robin stood to face Standing Arrow. "I can care for white dog alone," she retorted.

"Yellow Flower will care for her. You will get water and cook meals for both fires," Standing Arrow replied sternly.

Uncertain, Yellow Flower waited until Standing Arrow motioned her to Elizabeth's side. The medicine man had begun his chants and was standing over Elizabeth, shaking his rattle and prancing about. Yellow Flower immediately went to work cleansing and applying a mixture of herbs to Elizabeth's wound. With that done, Yellow Flower gently replaced the strips of buckskin to cover the injury.

The medicine man stopped abruptly when he finished his ritual, and silence filled the lodge. Yellow Flower quietly removed the heavy buffalo robe covering Elizabeth and began unbuttoning the front of her dress.

"Yellow Flower," said Standing Arrow, "I will be out by the fire. Call if you need me."

Nodding, Yellow Flower continued. After she took about two hours bathing Elizabeth's chest, stomach and face, the fever seemed to subside. Yellow Flower tucked the buffalo robe around her and called for Standing Arrow. "She will be fine for awhile. We must sleep," said Yellow Flower. She proceeded to lay down on a robe next to Elizabeth while Standing Arrow and Little Robin went to their own beds.

Morning came quickly, bringing a new day of sunshine. Elizabeth was improving under Yellow Flower's tender care, and Little Robin continued to provide meals for both Nakoma and Standing Arrow. Yellow Flower couldn't seem to get broth down Elizabeth without Standing Arrow's help. They worked together for two days wondering if she would be in her right mind when she came out of it.

Standing Arrow's heart felt tight when he looked at Elizabeth. The realization that Elizabeth would make him a good wife struck him hard. She was not out of danger yet. Would she live? Standing Arrow stayed at Elizabeth's side most of the time-watching and waiting.

By nightfall the second day, Elizabeth started tossing about trying to regain consciousness. When her eyes finally opened, she saw Standing Arrow gazing down at her and smiling. "My little Dove has returned," he murmured.

Bewildered, Yellow Flower looked at Standing Arrow, wondering what he had said to Elizabeth in her language.

Elizabeth looked around briefly, hastily assessing her whereabouts, as she heard Standing Arrow speaking to her.

Elizabeth regained her strength quickly and was able to sit up and move about easily within another two days. Little Robin still ignored her when Standing Arrow was not around.

But Yellow Flower was kind and gentle. Elizabeth wished she could talk with her. In the few days she had stayed with Elizabeth, smiles and nods-mixed with a little sign language—were all they could accomplish.

Yellow Flower went out early every morning to the dry meadows and harvested leaves from a falseboneset—or prairie wildflower-plant to make a fresh poultice to put on Elizabeth's swollen wound. She hung the yellow flowers from the plant in the tepee. Standing Arrow told Elizabeth that Yellow Flower had been give her name because as a child she picked yellow flowers to hang in the lodge or to tie in her hair.

Several times a day Yellow Flower made tea for Elizabeth from the leaves of the common yarrow plant to relieve the pain. Elizabeth didn't particularly like the taste, but with Yellow Flower urging her, she drank the tea. On the day Elizabeth ventured out of the lodge, Yellow Flower returned to her own lodge and her duties.

As the sun set that day, Elizabeth was sitting in her favorite spot by the stream. She hoped Standing Arrow would come and talk with her. Maybe he would answer some questions—if he would even speak to her. Elizabeth puzzled over his behavior the day she had approached him in camp.

Once again, Elizabeth did not hear him, but felt his presence next to her. They sat silently watching the last rays of light glisten across the water as it rippled slightly. Breaking the silence, Standing Arrow spoke in a deep tone of authority. "Your body has healing powers; you will be well soon."

Elizabeth turned to look at him as she spoke. "My power is from God." Pointing to the sky Elizabeth continued, "God helps me through all my troubles."

"God?" asked Standing Arrow. "Who is this God you speak of?"

Smiling, Elizabeth replied, "He is the Creator."

"You mean the Great Spirit?" questioned Standing Arrow.

"Well, yes, I guess that's what you might call him," replied Elizabeth.

Standing Arrow sat frowning in deep thought. Elizabeth changed the subject, thinking that was enough about God for one day. She would have to be careful and go slow when she told these people of God's love for every creature.

As Elizabeth spoke, Standing Arrow pushed the thoughts from his mind to listen to her speak. "Standing Arrow," Elizabeth said, "why would you not talk to me in the camp that day. I called out to you. Did you hear me?"

"Yes, I heard you." Elizabeth waited for him to explain. "It is a hard thing, I know, but it is the way of my people. If you stay you must earn the right to be spoken to," he continued.

Even more confused, Elizabeth said, "But you spoke to me in the lodge, and here by the stream. And what about Yellow Flower? She was kind to me."

"In one's own lodge a person can speak freely. I asked Yellow Flower to care for you," he replied.

"But now you're talking to me out here by the stream," retorted Elizabeth.

"It is dark and no one is out" replied Standing Arrow, shrugging his shoulders.

Exasperated, Elizabeth sighed. "What must I do to be accepted?"

"Each person's deeds are different," he stated. "You must do something big in the eyes of the people. Or if you shared my lodge, you would be accepted," the chief added with amusement.

"I do share your lodge," Elizabeth shot back, a question in her voice.

Standing Arrow nodded slowly. "Yes," he replied smiling, "but not my buffalo robe."

Shaken by the thought, Elizabeth quickly got to her feet and mumbled that it was time to get some sleep. She hurried back to the lodge and snuggled down under her buffalo robe.

Standing Arrow sat by the water's edge for a long time after Elizabeth left him. Deep in thought, he wondered at this white woman's reaction to him. If it had been any other young maiden in the village, wedding feast preparations would already be spoken of. He was not interested in any of the young girls that were in the village. Little Robin had tried several times to find him a wife, and each time he had refused. Standing Arrow decided that when his friend Trent came for a visit he would ask of the white man's ways and learn from him what he had done wrong.

Chapter Three

Elizabeth awoke feeling vibrant. The swelling had gone down, leaving only a little pain when she moved her arm. She praised the Lord that she had regained her strength so rapidly.

Elizabeth slipped silently out of the lodge. She decided to start the fire and heat some water. Picking up the bag she had seen Little Robin use, she headed for the stream. As she knelt and dipped the bag in the water, she wondered what it was made from. The outside was covered with deep wavy ridges. It almost resembled the underside of a large mushroom, but the inside was smooth and even. As Elizabeth pulled the heavy bag from the stream she strained because of having only one arm to use. But she easily managed to carry it back to camp.

Standing Arrow was scowling at her as she approached. "You should not carry water for a few more days," he said. "You will be sick again."

Smiling, Elizabeth said, "I feel wonderful; it won't hurt to do a little." Tipping her head slightly to one side and with an ornery twinkle in her eye she asked, "Did you forget you're not supposed to speak to me?"

Standing Arrow's eyes flashed angrily before he realized she was teasing him and with an unconcerned shrug of his shoulders he replied. "It is early; nobody will see."

"Well, since nobody will see," continued Elizabeth, "will you teach me to start a fire with that rock?"

Smiling, Standing Arrow gathered dry grass and leaves in a ball and began striking the steel that his white friend had brought to the Cheyenne village, against the flint. Tiny sparks flew out onto the grass and began smoldering. Standing Arrow picked the bundle up and began blowing softly on the embers until they leaped into flames. He then carefully placed more grass and small sticks over the flames until the fire crackled happily.

"Let me try that," Elizabeth asked as she gathered more dry grass and leaves. When she had enough, Standing Arrow handed her the flint and steel, showing her how to hold them and how to strike the steel with downward motions against the flint. Elizabeth tried and tried, but could not make a spark.

Amused, the chief watched as she tried over and over again. When frustration overtook her, she looked to him for help. Standing Arrow took Elizabeth's hands in his and struck the flint repeatedly, leaving little sprays of light with each stroke. When he thought she had the feel of it, he released her hands and she began again. Her

effort produced a few sparks and Elizabeth laughed happily as the tiny sparks jumped from the flint.

"Tomorrow we will try again," replied the young
chief.

When Little Robin emerged from the tepee, Elizabeth
was just dropping the rocks she had heated into the skin
pouch that served as a cooking pot. It was suspended on
a tripod of sticks and hung a few feet from the fire. Elizabeth noted that the inside of this pot looked the same as
the outside of the water bag. She must remember to ask
Standing Arrow what it was made from.

Little Robin hurried over to the fire to add more cold
rocks to the hot coals as she jabbered illegible words
that Elizabeth knew weren't kind. Sighing, Elizabeth ignored her and went into the woods to gather firewood.
At least there she wouldn't have to listen to Little Robin's
cruel chattering.

When Elizabeth returned with a load of wood, Yellow Flower was at the fire dipping hot liquid from the
pouch. Elizabeth was glad to see Yellow Flower, even if
she had to drink that awful tea. Looking up, Yellow
Flower saw Elizabeth carrying an armload of wood and
rushed to her side, taking the wood out of her arms and
jabbering words that Elizabeth didn't understand. But
Elizabeth sensed these words were of kindness and concern. She allowed Yellow Flower to fuss over her only
long enough to get the tea down and to show Yellow
Flower that her wound was much better.

After making a few more trips for wood, Elizabeth
was tired and realized she needed to rest before her
strength was completely gone.

The stream seemed to bring her comfort and, without realizing it, she headed to her favorite spot beside the waters.

Elizabeth awoke with a start as the pounding hooves and yipping of the warriors reached her ears. Scrambling to her feet, she watched as the cavalcade of horses and riders, Standing Arrow in the lead, approached the camp. Every warrior had meat hanging from his horse. They had had a successful hunt.

The camp came alive as the women began to butcher the carcasses. The men began their storytelling of the hunt, and the laughter and squeals of children filled the air.

Standing Arrow deposited a large buck in front of his mother. She spoke harsh, lashing, Cheyenne words to him. "If you would marry, I wouldn't have to do all the work."

Answering her, Standing Arrow replied hotly, "Teach Dove how to do the work." Although Elizabeth could not understand the words, she sensed they were talking about her. Little Robin confirmed that thought when she turned and spat at Elizabeth's feet, then angrily strode into the lodge.

The movement of Standing Arrow's jaw was visible anger. Elizabeth remained silent, not knowing what she should do.

Looking at the tepee door one more time, Standing Arrow came to a decision. He immediately went to work skinning the deer. It would be a disgrace to Little Robin that he did her work. Everyone in camp would know and it would not go well for her. Elizabeth watched as he quickly and skillfully removed the hide.

"I will teach you the ways of my people," stated Standing Arrow.

Elizabeth, eager to help and have someone speak to her, listened and watched carefully, helping when necessary. She asked questions about every part of the butchering process and was about to ask about the water pouch and cook pot when Standing Arrow removed the buck's stomach and handed it to Elizabeth. He told her to go and wash it in the stream and to make sure she was below the drinking spot. Elizabeth eagerly obeyed. As she rinsed the inside of the stomach, she began to see the funny texture appear. With a sickening realization, she knew what the water pot and cooking pot were made from.

Chapter Four

Daniel Mayfield sat in his overstuffed leather chair at the big oak desk in his library. He wondered why he had not received a telegram from Elizabeth. She should have arrived in Denver at least three weeks ago. She had promised to send a telegram as soon as she got there.

Daniel's thoughts were interrupted by a loud knock on the door. Quickly getting to his feet, he strode to the front door.

"Hello. Is this the Mayfield residence?" asked the delivery boy from the train station.

"Yes."

"I have three trunks in the wagon for you," stated the boy.

"Trunks!" Daniel cried as he abruptly walked past the boy and down to the wagon. Reaching the wagon, fear clutched his heart as he recognized Elizabeth's trunks.

"The trunks were sent back from Julesburg," said the boy.

"Sent back? Why?"

"I don't know, sir!"

Daniel quickly unloaded the trunks and carried them into the house, stopping only long enough to tell his wife, Ellen, what had arrived. He set a fast pace as he walked to the telegraph office across town.

The first telegram went to the older couple in Denver where Elizabeth was to be employed. He requested an immediate response and was prepared to wait a few hours for the message to be delivered and a return message sent. To his surprise, the return message came within forty-five minutes. Daniel supposed the couple must live close to the telegraph office to get such a quick response. Nervously Daniel read the message:

"Elizabeth Mayfield did not arrive STOP Charles and Clara Smith STOP"

The message was short and to the point. If Elizabeth didn't arrive, where could she be? Daniel remembered the delivery boy had said the trunks were sent back from Julesburg. He would send the next telegram to the stage station in Julesburg. With that task done, Daniel prepared for another long wait. Two hours passed slowly before the return message arrived:

"Stage attacked by Indians East of Julesburg STOP bodies of driver, shotgun guard and two male passengers were found STOP no sign of Elizabeth Mayfield's body STOP"

Daniel crumpled the message in his hand, while smashing a wicked blow to the desktop. "Those savage Indians captured her," he shouted aloud.

Tormenting thoughts flashed through his mind as he imagined the grotesque torture he had heard Indians did to captives—especially women. He must find out for sure if she was dead or if she was being kept alive and used for a slave. He prayed God would direct him with the search for his little girl. And if she was dead, he prayed she had died quickly and not a slow painful death.

Daniel walked home slowly to prolong having to share the news. He would have to tell Ellen and their youngest daughter, Katie. They would be devastated. It had been hard enough on them to have Elizabeth going to work in Denver. But dead or captured! How could he tell them? He wished he didn't have to tell them, but he knew he must.

Elizabeth stood shading her eyes as she watched Standing Arrow and Two Feathers ride into camp with two large bucks draped across their horses. Stopping in front of Elizabeth, Standing Arrow smiled. "We will have a camp feast."

As they moved on to the chief's lodge, Elizabeth wondered what a camp feast would be? The villagers had eaten their fill of venison last night. She wondered why they had brought more venison so soon.

Elizabeth watched the activities around her as the women built up fires and men cut large chunks of meat to be put on sticks over fires. Standing Arrow stopped and talked with Yellow Flower then proceeded to Elizabeth's side carrying both of the deerskins. "You will need a new dress soon. Yellow Flower will help you tan the hides," he stated.

Elizabeth looked over at the hide she and Standing Arrow had staked to the ground yesterday. Reading her thoughts, he replied, "Yes, you will need all three of them. I will help you stake them down. In the morning you can start scraping the first one." He was pleased that she seemed to accept the idea eagerly.

Elizabeth was not sure she would like a dress made of deerskin, but Standing Arrow was right. Her dress was in bad shape. She had felt Yellow Flower's dress before, and it was soft and supple, almost like flannel. The idea of a leather dress was intriguing.

As evening rolled around and the camp feast began, women brought different varieties of berries. Corn cakes were made, edible herbs and roots were boiled, and plenty of venison was cooked. Elizabeth enjoyed the meal, even though Yellow Flower and Standing Arrow were the only ones that acknowledged she was there.

Yellow Flower taught Elizabeth some of the dance steps as the drums beat and the women chanted, slowly moving in a circle around the fire. Elizabeth wasn't sure what it all meant, but felt she must participate. Standing Arrow nodded approvingly as she circled in front of him. The women swayed and swirled to the beat of the music, leaving a soft tinkle from the shells on their dresses, like a whisper of leaves on a windy day.

The repetitious pounding of the drums went on late into the night. Small children, sleeping on buffalo robes around the fire, were scattered among adults. Elizabeth finally dragged herself to bed. She was exhausted and sleep claimed her quickly.

When the sun arose and shone down on the Cheyenne camp, most of the villagers were sound asleep, and would be for some time. The camp slowly came alive with children running and shouting, woman dipping water and men caring for horses. Elizabeth awoke, remembering she was supposed to scrape the first hide today. Yellow Flower would most likely spend the day with her. With that thought a smile played at her lips.

She liked Yellow Flower and was anxious to learn from her. Elizabeth also hoped Yellow Flower would be willing to learn some English. She would start slowly, only a few words each time they worked together. Yellow Flower was the only friend she had here among the Cheyenne, and Elizabeth intended to learn the ways of her people quickly.

She was already able to understand some conversations. Even if she didn't understand each word, she caught the thoughts and intents of conversations. Speaking the language would take much longer. Suddenly, Elizabeth wondered why she was thinking about learning their language. Surely the white trapper would be coming soon and she would go back to civilization with him. But how long would that be?

Elizabeth decided she would learn as much as she could while she was here. Standing Arrow would be pleased. She liked the twinkle in his dark eyes when she pleased him—and the half smile that tugged at one corner of his lips. There her thoughts went again. Why should she care about what he thought? She was leaving here as soon as she could. Her father would be worried sick by now since he would not have received a telegram from her.

Elizabeth stepped out of the lodge. Looking toward the heavens, she prayed for guidance and protection as she faced the day. She also took time each day to praise God for all his love and mercy and for sending his Son to die on Calvary so she could be saved. She prayed God would use her to show these Cheyenne Indians their need for salvation.

Elizabeth quoted John 3:16 to herself: *For God so loved the world, that he gave his only begotten Son, that whosoever believeth in him should not perish, but have everlasting life.* She knew that Jesus died for the Cheyenne people and he wanted to see them saved. If she had been put here to be used by God, she didn't want to fail. Therefore, she must learn their ways and language.

The day spent with Yellow Flower was pleasant. To Elizabeth's delight, Yellow Flower enjoyed learning words. They took turns pointing to objects and repeating the unfamiliar words. After awhile they both laughed and started over. By the time Yellow Flower had instructed her and helped her scrape the hair from the first hide, both had learned several words including words about scraping the deer hide.

The next day was much like the previous one, except Yellow Flower scraped one hide while Elizabeth scraped the other. They continued to learn each other's language daily, and even if they didn't work together, they made time each day to go over the words.

Yellow Flower continued to help Elizabeth when she tanned the hide. She showed Elizabeth how to heat and mix the brains of the deer with enough water, smashing it into a thin paste and applying the mixture to the hide. After the brains dried, the hides were ready to be worked until they were soft and supple.

"Next, they must hang in the tepee for several days to allow the smoke to penetrate through them," explained Standing Arrow to Elizabeth. "The smoke keeps them from turning hard again." Elizabeth wasn't sure she understood, but watched as Standing Arrow used a rawhide rope to hoist the hides to the top of the tepee.

Yellow Flower came early the fourth day ready to help Elizabeth make her dress. Smiling, Yellow Flower asked Elizabeth in English, "Sew dress?"

Elizabeth smiled and nodded as she said, "Sew dress," in Cheyenne. The two young women laughed and hugged each other.

Standing Arrow emerged from the lodge carrying the hides, just in time to hear Little Robin mutter her hateful remarks about Elizabeth. He threw her a reprimanding glance as he handed Elizabeth the three deerskins.

Yellow Flower and Elizabeth didn't seem to notice Little Robin's remarks as they prepared themselves to work. Yellow Flower chose the hide for the top. She began by cutting a hole in the middle of it, just the right size to go over Elizabeth's head. During the next step the women faced each other as they sewed another hide to the side of the top piece, leaving several inches to be cut into fringe. They then cut the fringe up each side of the dress, using the fringe to tie the dress together instead of sewing up the sides. Cutting the fringe was tiresome and took most of the day, but by nightfall the dress was together.

Yellow Flower had brought over four small shells and sewed them across the front. Elizabeth thought the little shells were very pretty and added a delicate touch to the golden skins. She thanked Yellow Flower with a hug and returned to the lodge proudly carrying her new dress.

Standing Arrow knew Elizabeth had finished her dress. He was anxious to see if she would wear it right away or if she would wait until her other dress could no longer be worn. Sighing, he knew he had to go on the hunt early and would have to wait until he got back to see.

The warriors left in two groups. Standing Arrow took seven braves with him and headed east. Black Crow and his men rode west until they knew the chief couldn't see them and then quickly detoured to the south. Black Crow and his men were looking for scalps.

They had been denied the scalp of the pretty white woman, but this time they wouldn't bring back prisoners. Standing Arrow would be mad. He had told them not to attack and kill the white man unless the white man attacked first. But Black Crow would think of something to tell Standing Arrow before they got back to camp.

After a successful hunt, the hunting party returned to camp mid-morning. Riding into the village, Standing Arrow scanned it, hoping to see Elizabeth. Soon the village women happily gathered around the warriors and took the meat from them. The chief handed a portion to Little Robin, who hurried away to take care of the venison. He looked around camp and noticed that Yellow Flower was not around either. So he decided the women must be together and set out to find them.

When he spotted them in the woods, he quietly moved closer. His heart filled with pride as he saw that Elizabeth was wearing the new dress. Her blonde hair was parted and neatly braided. Each braid was tied with strips of buckskin.

Yellow Flower was showing Elizabeth plants and animal signs as they walked along. Elizabeth picked a purple flower and stuck it in her braid while Yellow Flower searched and found a yellow blossom to put in hers. Standing Arrow watched, amused as the pair rambled through the woods like children at play. When it came time to return to camp Standing Arrow slipped back unseen.

After the evening meal Elizabeth went to relax by the stream and to watch the sun slip slowly beyond the horizon. Standing Arrow approached quietly. "You are happy here?" he asked.

Startled, Elizabeth jumped and responded too quickly. "No, I want to go home." Elizabeth could see the disappointment in the young chief's eyes, but he didn't voice it. Elizabeth felt bad for answering so harshly. She wasn't exactly unhappy; she just missed her family. With that thought Elizabeth realized that if she were in Denver she would miss them too.

"You look Cheyenne in the buckskins," Standing Arrow stated solemnly.

"Thank you," replied Elizabeth, looking down at her dress. She was hoping that was a compliment. Elizabeth detected a note of discouragement in his voice as they spoke. She thought Standing Arrow wanted to say more to her, but she couldn't break the tension between them. The silence of the night pressed heavy upon them as they sat side by side watching the water glisten in the moonlight. Both were buried in their own thoughts, and unable to put them into words.

⊰⊱

Black Crow and his men rode steadily all day, stopping only long enough to eat and let the horses rest. The next day the warriors scoured the valleys and hills looking for plunder. The small war party topped a rise that overlooked a large valley. Black Crow halted the group. Pointing across the valley to the tree line, he smiled cruelly. A small group of Commanches slowly threaded their way through the trees. Eagerly, Black Crow's party descended on the unsuspecting victims. Snake was the first to let an arrow fly and the rest simultaneously followed his lead.

The raid ended as quickly as it had begun. The five Cheyenne warriors greedily took six scalps from the elderly, the wounded and some young children. Carelessly, they left arrows that told the plains who had done this ghastly deed. Proud of their raid, the warriors headed north, looking for more excitement.

Later in the day they stumbled onto two young bucks, apparently on their vision quest to become men. The war party overtook and ruthlessly destroyed them, taking only their scalps and leaving the condemning evidence behind. Picking up the pace, Black Crow knew it was time to go back to camp.

The warriors remained happy and jovial as they made the trek back. Only Black Crow thought of what he would tell Standing Arrow. The chief would be angry and Black Crow would be responsible for what the war party did. If they kept moving they would make camp before daylight. Black Crow planned to slip into camp without waking anyone.

When they reached camp, he instructed the warriors to move slowly and quietly. Each one slunk toward his own lodge. Black Crow rounded his lodge to be greeted by the tall chief. Black Crow unconsciously backed up a few steps.

"Where have you been?" demanded Standing Arrow. "And why do you carry fresh scalps at your belt?"

Unprepared to face him, Black Crow hastily replied, "We were attacked."

Glaring at him, Standing Arrow said doubtfully, "And you have no battle wounds?"

Black Crow lifted his chin and leveled his gaze to meet Standing Arrow's disapproving look. "We fight like men," he said thickly as he pounded his protruding chest. "We are Cheyenne warriors. Our enemies, the Commanche, are weak. We hear them coming."

Unconvinced of Black Crow's story, Standing Arrow sternly reminded him, "If you are not careful you will start a war among the tribes, and the village would be attacked. Women and children would be killed and your scalp will then dangle from a Commanche belt." Standing Arrow turned sharply and strode away into the darkness.

Black Crow knew this was true but kept pushing it further back into his mind, until the lie seemed more like truth than the truth. He would show Standing Arrow. He would bring in more scalps; the people would see that he was a great warrior. They would take his side. Nothing would stop him.

———

Elizabeth and Yellow Flower left camp early to pick wild strawberries. The best strawberry patch was an hour walk from camp. Elizabeth enjoyed the morning air and the time spent with Yellow Flower. She was learning more and more of their language and could even speak a few phrases. She had tried to talk to Yellow Flower about God, but she didn't feel like she knew enough Cheyenne to explain it. Yellow Flower believed in a Great Spirit but could not understand anything beyond that. Elizabeth told her that God loved her and sent his Son to die on the cross so she could go to heaven, if she'd just ask him into her heart. Yellow Flower looked at Elizabeth with confusion and worry on her brow. Thinking that maybe Elizabeth's fever had gone too high or that it was returning, she instinctively reached up to feel Elizabeth's forehead. With a sigh, Elizabeth changed the subject, but she silently prayed God would allow her to reach Yellow Flower.

Black Crow was up early and had seen Yellow Flower and Elizabeth leave camp carrying baskets. With a vindictive grin, he decided to follow them. Thinking he was unobserved, he edged his way into the trees and walked silently along the path. Standing Arrow and Nakoma had also watched the young women leave, trailed by Black Crow.

Waiting only a few short minutes, Standing Arrow and Nakoma moved swiftly through the woods, keeping a safe distance between Black Crow and themselves.

Unaware of other watchful eyes, Black Crow sat silently watching the young women pick strawberries. He was trying to devise a plan to separate them just long enough for him to get his hands on the white woman.

With their baskets filled to the brim, Elizabeth and Yellow Flower hurried along the path toward camp. Black Crow stayed close behind waiting to seize any opportunity that came.

Standing Arrow and Nakoma moved swiftly on ahead where the trail narrowed and the girls would have to walk single file. The chief knew this would be where Black Crow would make his move.

Yellow Flower stepped in front of Elizabeth as they made their way on the narrow trail. Danger could be lurking around every corner and Yellow Flower, more accustomed to the wilderness, always led the way. Most days the pair walked slowly, enjoying time together. But today Yellow Flower seemed edgy. Elizabeth noticed her friend had hurried while picking strawberries, wanting to return quickly to camp. She had even started back at a brisk pace.

When they reached the narrow trail, Yellow Flower warily scanned the area. Taking Elizabeth's hand, she stepped out in the lead. A few short steps farther, Yellow Flower stopped and listened to the hawk call. The call meant nothing to Elizabeth, but Yellow Flower knew instantly it was a warning from Nakoma. Dropping her basket, she grabbed Elizabeth by the hand and broke into a run.

Black Crow had not known that the hawk call was Nakoma. When the girls began to run, he made his move. Jumping from cover, he seized Elizabeth. He grabbed her from behind. His powerful arm held her neck in a deadly grip as he firmly pressed a knife against her throat.

Yellow Flower, knowing Nakoma was close, let go of Elizabeth's hand and drew her own knife, preparing to aid her friend. Black Crow laughed wickedly as he pulled Elizabeth backward, away from Yellow Flower.

Standing Arrow and Nakoma, crouched like mountain lions waiting for the right instant to pounce on their prey, were behind Black Crow.

Elizabeth struggled violently to free herself from Black Crow's clutches. Yellow Flower, seeing the warriors, spoke a warning to Elizabeth in English. Immediately Elizabeth ceased struggling, knowing it would be easier for her rescuers if she remained still. Black Crow, wary of Yellow Flower's words that brought a calm to his captive, began to search for a quick getaway. He had not thought to bring a horse, and he knew Yellow Flower would be trouble. She was as able to use that knife as most warriors were. Fearing she might try to throw it, he hurried farther into the woods, dragging Elizabeth along.

As Black Crow reached a thick clump of trees, Standing Arrow and Nakoma seized him on either side. Standing Arrow wrenched Elizabeth from Black Crow's grasp while Nakoma twisted Black Crow's arms unmercifully behind him, tying his wrists with rawhide strips.

Standing Arrow helped Elizabeth to her feet. She smiled shakily and thanked him for saving her from "that animal."

"That is two times I save you from him," he said with a twinkle in his eyes.

"Yes, it is," replied Elizabeth.

Returning to their hastily dropped baskets, the girls made short work of refilling them and headed back to camp.

Standing Arrow and Nakoma roughly escorted Black Crow along the trail. He would be punished for this deed, but not severely enough Standing Arrow feared.

The council met that very evening. All the men assembled around a big roaring fire in the center of the camp. The talk continued late, and Elizabeth wondered if the drums would ever stop throbbing in her head. They were like an outward heartbeat that would only stop upon death.

With the last beat of the drum, the council was over. A decision had been reached. Standing Arrow returned to the lodge with a grim report. Sitting beside Elizabeth on the buffalo robe, he told her all that had happened. "The council chose to free him, you are not a member of the tribe and therefore he did not break a tribal law," he concluded. She had expected this, but had hoped the chief could sway their decision.

Standing Arrow lifted her chin to meet his gaze. She saw concern in his eyes that startled her. She now realized the new danger her life was in.

"You must not leave the camp without me!" ordered Standing Arrow. Elizabeth did not respond, but looked away. "My little Dove is stubborn, but if she wants to stay alive she will obey," he said flatly.

Elizabeth knew she would obey, but she didn't like the idea one bit. *Maybe,* she thought, *I could learn the skills of a knife-thrower or how to use a bow and arrow.* She would rid herself of this problem! Sighing, she knew she could never do that. She would rely on the Lord to take care of her. Reciting First Peter 3:12 and 13 to herself gave her courage. *For the eyes of the Lord are over the righteous, and his ears are open unto their prayer: but the face of the Lord is against them that do evil. And who is he that will harm you, if ye be followers of that which is good?*

Chapter Five

Daniel Mayfield worked methodically each day to tie up the loose strings of his life in the East, while his wife and daughter sorted and packed, choosing only a few treasures and a limited supply of necessities.

Ellen wasn't sure she wanted to move west, but Daniel had wanted to go years ago when they had first begun their life together. She knew a part of him had left with Elizabeth.

Katie was overjoyed with the thought of adventure, and bubbled as she sorted and packed. She seemed to have a perfect peace that they would find Elizabeth and everything would be fine. Both Daniel and Ellen knew the chances of finding Elizabeth were slim, but something tugged at their hearts. It gave them hope.

When her parents had gently tried to tell her that Elizabeth might not be alive, Katie had reminded them of Jesus' words in Mark 9:23: *"If thou canst believe, all things are possible to him that believeth."* Sighing, Ellen had given up trying to talk to Katie. As time went on Katie knew they all would realize that it just didn't hurt as much if you thought there might be a chance Elizabeth was alive.

While the last trunks were being loaded on the train, the Mayfield family anxiously waited for the boarding call. Daniel had sold their spacious house and general store in two short weeks and had a large sum of money to start over nicely in the West. He had dreamed of going west since he was fourteen and could hardly believe it was really happening. He knew Ellen liked the comfort of the city—the stores and tea parties, church and neighbors—and was scared to live in the Wild West. But, she would have to adjust her thinking.

Daniel didn't know how long it would take to find Elizabeth—or information about her—but he would hunt until he found her or knew for certain that she was dead. Daniel decided he would find a nice house in Julesburg and quickly settle the women before he headed to the mountains.

"Papa, are you coming?" Katie was pulling on his sleeve.

"Yes," Daniel answered, shaking off his thoughts and returning to the present. "I'm all set; let's go." Daniel reached down to pick up the valise containing items they would need to endure the long train ride.

Climbing aboard, Ellen couldn't resist looking back to take a quick scan of the town. Halfway through, she realized Lot's wife had done that, and God had turned

her into a pillar of salt. Quickly turning, she boarded the
train without looking back again. She was going west with
her husband, and she would make the best of it. Ellen was
determined not be a hindrance to him. Her place was with
her husband; she would go and not look back. A new beginning, a new town, a new life.

As the train chugged and built up speed, Ellen's heart
began to spark with excitement. No longer worried or
scared, she would lean on God to help her in times of
doubt. She remembered the sermon Preacher Yount had
given a few months back about worry. He had read scripture from Matthew 6:25–34: *"Therefore I say unto you,
Take no thought for your life, what ye shall eat, or what ye
shall drink; nor yet for your body, what ye shall put on. Is not
the life more than meat, and the body than raiment? Behold
the fowls of the air: for they sow not, neither do they reap, nor
gather into barns; yet your heavenly Father feedeth them. Are
ye not much better than they? Which of you by taking thought
can add one cubit unto his stature? And why take ye thought
for raiment? Consider the lilies of the field, how they grow;
they toil not, neither do they spin: And yet I say unto you,
That even Solomon in all his glory was not arrayed like one of
these. Wherefore, if God so clothe the grass of the field, which
to day is, and to morrow is cast into the oven, shall he not
much more clothe you, O ye of little faith? Therefore take no
thought, saying, What shall we eat? or, What shall we drink?
or, Wherewithal shall we be clothed? (For after all these things
do the Gentiles seek:) for your heavenly Father knoweth that
ye have need of all these things. But seek ye first the kingdom
of God, and his righteousness; and all these things shall be*

added unto you. Take therefore no thought for the morrow: for the morrow shall take thought for the things of itself. Sufficient unto the day is the evil thereof."

⚬⚬⚬

Elizabeth stayed close to the lodge, as Standing Arrow had instructed. She only ventured as far away as the stream—and then only if it was daylight. The weeks dragged by more slowly now and Elizabeth spent more time tanning hides, preparing jerky and sewing.

Yellow Flower was teaching her to sew beautiful designs on leather bags and dresses using colorful porcupine quills. Elizabeth was unhappy when Yellow Flower went without her into the woods in search of roots and plants to use for dyeing the quills.

She had tried to convince Standing Arrow to let her go, but he had refused. Disappointed and angry, Elizabeth sat in front of the lodge for several hours moping and feeling sorry for herself. She missed her family so much. Would she ever see them again? Thoughts of escape crept into her mind and slowly grew into a powerful desire. *Why not?* she'd ask herself.

The reason for staying was the fear of Black Crow coming after her in the woods. And now she feared him here in camp. She didn't like the thought of Standing Arrow being angry with her, and if she left in the night she wouldn't be able to say good-bye. Elizabeth knew he would be hurt and angry.

She also knew she couldn't bear this kind of confinement much longer. She loved going into the forest to search for plants and watch the animals scurry about. She liked to sit in the grass among the trees and listen to the leaves whisper to each other. It was a good place to be alone and talk to God. She could think more clearly and find peace-yes, perfect peace, the kind of peace promised in Isaiah 26:3: *"Thou wilt keep him in perfect peace, whose mind is stayed on thee: because he trusteth in thee."*

She was thankful that Standing Arrow occasionally took time to escort her into the forest. Although she did enjoy the time she was allowed to spend in the woods, she felt she couldn't just sit under the trees and think for long periods of time, expecting Standing Arrow to wait for her.

Sighing, Elizabeth watched for Yellow Flower to appear at the edge of the forest since it was about time for her to return. As Elizabeth scanned the last clump of trees, she saw Yellow Flower trudging along slowly. She was carrying a basket with plants and roots piled high. They poked out in every direction. Jumping to her feet, Elizabeth closed the space between them quickly. When she took the basket from Yellow Flower, Elizabeth noticed how tired she looked, something she hadn't noticed before. Yellow Flower's eyes were rimmed with dark circles and her face looked haggard. Elizabeth wondered if she was sick, but Yellow Flower assured her she would be fine. *I'll keep an eye on her,* Elizabeth thought.

As they walked together, Elizabeth stole glances at her friend every few seconds, trying to decide what was wrong with Yellow Flower. Standing still, Yellow Flower looked the same. But as they walked, her dress flounced back just enough to expose a nicely rounded stomach. Elizabeth gasped with excitement and reached out to touch Yellow Flower's stomach. "Why didn't you tell me you were going to have a baby?"

With a half grin, Yellow Flower responded, "I wasn't sure you would be happy for me!"

"Why wouldn't I be happy?"

"It will mean more duties," replied Yellow Flower.

Realizing that Yellow Flower was trying to tell her she wouldn't be able to spend as much time with her, Elizabeth hugged her and reassured her that she understood. "I'd love to help with the baby and the extra duties."

Both girls smiled brightly as they continued through camp to Yellow Flower's lodge, chattering the whole way. Wistfully, Elizabeth told Yellow Flower that she loved babies and would like to have a family of her own. When she realized she hadn't asked when the baby would be born, she blurted out her question.

"In the season of great snow." Yellow Flower's voice had a tone of dread in it. Elizabeth knew this would be a hard time for a new life to enter the world, but she was sure Nakoma was a good husband who would help her with her duties. Elizabeth didn't consider that she might not be there to help her friend.

The girls continued working throughout the day, dyeing and sorting quills. They were preparing enough quills to last through the cold winter months. During those months, they would sit by the fire and sew the porcupine quills to soft deer hides that had been tanned and made into a variety of items to be used by their family members.

Elizabeth was amazed how the roots and flowers produced such vivid colors as they changed the quills from white to shades of radiant yellow or orange. The berries they found turned the quills a nice purple and a deep red. The girls were anxious to start their projects. Yellow Flower was working on an intricate design on a cradle board.

Elizabeth was sewing basic designs on a bag for her first quill project. She had also made a small bag from soft flank leather that she sewed inside her buckskin dress. In it she placed the only items she had left from her personal belongings: three twenty-dollar gold pieces, a broach that had belonged to her grandmother, and a small cross on a gold chain that Katie had given her.

She had left the items hidden in the secret pocket that had been sewn shut on the inside of her cotton dress until she finished the leather bag. It was a comfort to have them with her at all times. Although she was glad she still had these precious items, she really wished she had a Bible. She missed reading God's Word, and although she did recite scripture everyday, she still longed to read the Bible and listen to God through his Word.

Elizabeth had finally made Yellow Flower understand that God was what the Cheyenne thought of as the "Great Spirit." She was still trying to help Standing Arrow understand that, but he would listen for just so long, wrinkle his forehead, get up and walk away. She had accomplished a great deal, but still had a long way to go.

⸻

Using the last of the flour and coffee, the young mountain man decided it was time to go down into town and stock up for the long winter months. With this decision made, he wasted no time preparing. He would start out this morning and go to the Cheyenne village for a few weeks before he went into Julesburg. Trent packed his bedroll, a small amount of clothing and a sparse bundle for cooking while he traveled.

Gathering the best of his mangy summer pelts, he hoped they would bring enough money to lay in supplies. He strapped them to the pack mule along with his personal gear and the few camping supplies he'd need. He took down the lean—to that served as his home and quickly packed up the rest of his gear. Carrying the items carefully, he positioned them so they didn't take up much space in a nearby long-abandoned coyote den. After stowing his belongings there, he carefully covered the opening with branches and roots in order to conceal the objects inside.

When he was satisfied, he picked up his flintlock rifle and climbed aboard his black mare. The mare was eager to go and started at a good pace but soon tired of the constant pull from the pack mule, which made her slow to a steady plodding. Trent also was eager, and encouraged the pack mule along with a hard tug on the lead every once in awhile. But at last he settled in with the mare's steady plodding.

Spotting a small war party in the distance, he drew up among the trees that skirted the valley. He wanted to allow them plenty of time to pass. Since he didn't know if they where friendly or hostile, he decided it would be wise to wait. His judgment proved to be good. Their faces were painted for war and they were heavily armed.

When the danger was past, he proceeded toward the Cheyenne village.

Just before dusk, he spotted the tops of many tepees. As he topped the rise, he could see the entire village. He always loved the view from this rise. The tepees stood majestically against the sky. Their tops were dark from the smoke that lazily rolled out to meet the setting sun. The stream wound gracefully along the edge of camp. Children ran about playing, and horses stood feeding contently. Trent nudged the mare on. Riding to the large tepee in the center of camp, he hailed the lodge as he dismounted. Emerging from the lodge, Standing Arrow welcomed his friend. Little Robin quickly brought food to Trent and smiling happily at his arrival. As Trent ate, he told Standing Arrow about the Commanche war party he had seen in the area and the signs of a small buffalo herd nearby.

Eager to hunt together, the chief and the mountain man made plans to leave in the morning to trail the buffalo. The village needed a good supply of meat and hides for the approaching winter. Warriors from each lodge would be included in this hunt. It would most likely be the last big hunt before winter.

The talk of old friends continued over the firelight for many hours. Just as Trent began to ask Standing Arrow why Little Robin was so happy to see him, he caught sight of Elizabeth rounding the tepee. Even in the darkness he could tell she was a white woman—a very pretty white woman-dressed in Cheyenne buckskins. Standing Arrow followed Trent's gaze until his eyes rested on Elizabeth entering the chief's lodge. With a heavy heart Standing Arrow stated, "She is a brave one."

Puzzled, Trent asked, "Why is she here?"

"She was captured by Black Crow and his warriors. I would not allow them to kill her. She was brave, and earned the right to live."

"Did you take her for your wife?" asked Trent.

"No," spat Standing Arrow hastily.

"You did not want her?" Although relieved that Standing Arrow had not forced the white woman to marry him, Trent was shocked.

Standing Arrow got to his feet angrily. "I want, but she does not want me," he hissed as he pounded a fist to his massive chest and strode into the darkness.

Inside the tepee, Elizabeth had heard the exchange between the two friends. Even though they spoke in Cheyenne, she understood every word that had been spoken. When she had walked up to the fire, she had not noticed who was sitting at the fire with Standing Arrow since she never approached him unless he was alone.

Everyone in the village knew Standing Arrow talked with Elizabeth, but she knew it would be better to be silent around others. Had she realized before entering the lodge that Standing Arrow's guest was the white man, she would have approached him. Hearing Standing Arrow stalk off into the night, she quietly lifted the door of the lodge and eagerly slipped out.

She was standing at Trent's side and spoke to him before he heard her. "Hello."

Startled, he turned to face her. "Howdy ma'am,"

"I've been waiting for you to come."

"You have?"

"Yes, Standing Arrow said you would take me back to a town!" replied Elizabeth.

"Are you being treated good?" asked Trent with concern in his voice.

"Oh yes, very well-except that no one talks to me. I have one friend who has taught me the Cheyenne ways. Little Robin hates me and will be glad to see me go!"

Trent now knew why Little Robin was so glad to see him. She had been sharing her lodge with this white woman reluctantly. "What is your name, ma'am?" he asked.

"Elizabeth-Elizabeth Mayfield. And you are Trent?"

"Yes, ma'am."

"I'm so glad you finally came. I was about to give up on you."

"That young chief is mighty fond of you ma'am!"

Elizabeth felt like Trent could see right through to her soul as he eyed her. Uneasy, she replied, "Yes I . . . I think he is."

"Good night ma'am," Trent said softly as he picked up his bedroll and walked toward the trees.

Elizabeth felt lonely and cold. She wanted to sit by the stream with Standing Arrow, but she thought he might not want her company tonight. Trent wasn't exactly talkative, and she certainly didn't want to go into the tepee with Little Robin. The stream won out.

She hurried across camp, knowing she wasn't supposed to be out alone. She slowed only when she was near the spot where she knew Standing Arrow would be. Quietly and very slowly, she crept closer so Standing Arrow wouldn't hear her. Pleased with herself that she had not made a sound, she settled in to wait until he went back to camp.

"You make much noise," stated Standing Arrow dryly.

So she hadn't been quiet after all. Disappointed, Elizabeth wondered how he knew it was her and not an animal or another person. He was sitting with his back to her and he hadn't moved or turned his head.

Quickly moving to his side, she resettled herself and sat quietly. The beauty of the evening seemed to go unnoticed as the two sat lost in their own thoughts, each wondering what the future would bring. Both knew Elizabeth would be leaving soon.

The shimmering twinkle of the stars and the bright moon seemed dull and far away tonight. Standing Arrow had hoped Elizabeth would stay and be his wife. But it was obvious she was eager to leave. His time spent with Trent would not be fun now—not when Trent would take Elizabeth away, back to her people. Standing Arrow sat brooding for hours, as the darkness closed in around them.

Elizabeth also was sad-sad that she had to choose one way of life over the other. Sad, too, that she had not been able to win these people to the truth and understanding of her Lord and Savior. But maybe her job was just to plant the seeds of salvation and someone else would water and harvest them.

Rising abruptly, Standing Arrow spoke "It is time to return to camp. I must leave early with many warriors and women to hunt the buffalo."

Elizabeth had been with the Cheyenne long enough to know that the women went only to work. It was a long tiresome job to dry all the meat before packing it back to the village, and only the women worthy of such a task were permitted to go. The women chosen were the hardest workers and the most dedicated women. Without hesitating about the work, Elizabeth asked, "Can I go with you?"

"No," snapped Standing Arrow, not even giving her working abilities a thought. "You must stay at the village where you are safe."

"I would be safe with you and all your warriors," pleaded Elizabeth.

"No."

Crushed, Elizabeth said no more

Moving along the path soundlessly, they made their way back to camp and into the large tepee. Little Robin greeted them with an ugly scowl of disapproval. Elizabeth, unable to sleep, decided she would talk to Yellow Flower in the morning, before the men left. She was sure Yellow Flower was one of the women who would be going with them.

As soon as Standing Arrow left the lodge early the next morning to prepare for the hunt, Elizabeth slipped out unnoticed and went to Yellow Flower's lodge. When Elizabeth told her what she planned to do, Yellow Flower was sure Standing Arrow would be angry. Both of them knew it would infuriate Standing Arrow if Elizabeth went with the hunting party. She reminded Elizabeth it was not a good thing to make the chief angry.

When Yellow Flower was convinced that Elizabeth would not change her mind, she agreed to help, but only by loaning her a blanket. The morning air was chilly, so Elizabeth wrapped the blanket over her head and around her body, making it impossible to tell who she was. She made certain she did not ride close to Yellow Flower, for fear that Standing Arrow would realize who she was.

As the day wore on and the sun traveled higher in the sky, Elizabeth realized they were far enough away from the village that Standing Arrow wouldn't send her back now. When she could bear the heat of the blanket no longer and was about to remove it, the men sighted the buffalo herd.

Wheeling his horse around, Standing Arrow instructed the small group of women to set up camp. With that said the men rode off.

Chapter Six

The stage rumbled and bounced over the rutted road, stirring up a thick dust that engulfed the stage and settled on the passengers. Ellen wondered if she would ever breathe fresh air again.

At the stop before Julesburg, Daniel ask the grizzled old driver to show him the spot where the Indians had attacked the stage early that spring.

With a sideways glance the driver asked, "Ya kin ta one of them that them Injuns kilt?"

"Yes," replied Daniel. "My daughter was on that stage, but no sign of her body was found. I'm going up in the hills to find her."

The leathered old man swung his gaze to meet Daniel's in disbelief. "Only a fool er a tenderfoot would go traipsing around in them there mountains, crawlin' with Injuns an wild animals."

Daniel chuckled softly. "I plan to hire a man to travel with me. One that knows the country and can speak with the Indians."

"Yar wastin' yor time. I'm right sorry about yor gal, but ifen and I mean if she is alive, you cain't just go waltzing in and take her," protested the driver.

"I need to know if she is alive or dead. The uncertainty is worse that death. I must try." Daniel spoke with emotion.

Shaking his head, the driver walked back to the coach muttering out loud, "What a shame . . . tenderfoot . . . crazy fool gonna git himself kilt."

Daniel kept his remarks to himself as he climbed aboard the coach. Fresh thoughts of his eldest daughter in the hands of savages swept over him, leaving him nauseated. As the day wore on, Daniel began to relax. Katie was so full of assurance and babbled on about seeing Elizabeth again. Daniel had almost forgotten she was lost to them in a vast unknown land.

They had bounced and jarred along for a few miles when the speed of the stage rapidly decreased. "Whooooa!" Charlie hollered to the horses. The passengers pitched around inside the coach as it came to a sudden halt. Charlie had been driving stages for years and he never stopped unless it was very important. His stages were always on time, and he aimed to keep it that way.

He wasn't sure this was important, but the sadness in Mr. Mayfield's eyes had twisted the old driver's insides. "Whooaa!" he hollered again as he jumped down from the seat above. "Tenderfoot," he called as he opened the door, "thar tis, the stage was right thar when we

70

found it. The Injuns came down from that ridge, pointing toward it as he spoke. They never had a chance. Kilt em all."

"Not all," replied Daniel sternly. "They never found my daughter."

Climbing quickly aboard, Charlie slapped the reins across the team's backs and they thundered down the trail.

Julesburg was not a large town, but it did have adequate stores to provide the townspeople and folks on surrounding ranches with the supplies they needed. As the stage rolled to a stop, the dust settled. Ellen and Katie looked around anxiously. Ellen was the first to notice the steeple on the little white church at the edge of town. She sighed contentedly, knowing there was a church here. She vowed she would make her husband proud of her. She would make friends and settle into life in the west. As they climbed down from the long tiresome stage ride, Ellen was glad she had finally agreed to come west. Daniel had wanted this ever since they had first met.

Their trunks were quickly unloaded and the stage moved on. Daniel checked his family into the hotel. While they rested, he began planning his next moves. First he would ask around about a house, then he would need to find a guide and outfit himself with what he and the guide would need to go find Elizabeth.

The day was almost gone. He would have to wait until morning to start his house search. The Mayfields ate supper at the local cafe, spending most of their evening visiting with Mary, the waitress, and a few townspeople. By the end of the evening they had found a few leads on houses for sale and Katie had been proposed to by a young cowpuncher.

Mr. Davis, one of the town's businessmen, told Daniel he had ridden in the posse that went after Elizabeth. He regretted that the search had been abandoned, and had often thought about that poor girl being a prisoner. Excitedly, Daniel asked Mr. Davis if he had seen Elizabeth with the Indians when they were trailing them.

"No, we didn't actually see her. We were a good day behind, but we saw where they stopped and got water. She was with them all right," Mr. Davis reported, shaking his head sadly.

"I'm going after her," stated Daniel flatly.

"What? Alone in that wild country? You've got to be crazy. You'll get yourself killed."

"I'm looking to hire someone to take me, someone that can talk to the Indians," replied Daniel.

Mr. Davis shook his head thoughtfully. "I know a young mountain man that lives up there, but he only comes to town a few times each year. He knows the Cheyenne. He spends time at their village. He should be coming to town any time now. Ask at the general store if he's been in. His name is Trent. Don't know the last name, but they'll know who your talking about."

"Thanks," replied Daniel as they stood to leave the cafe.

In the morning Daniel slipped out of the room without disturbing his family. He planned to find the houses Mr. Davis had told him about. By doing that before the women awoke, he could take them directly to the houses and save time hunting for the addresses.

He found a large white house within a few blocks of the center of town that he was sure Ellen and Katie would fall in love with. It had a white picket fence all the way around the yard and lots of flowers. It also had a big porch with a hanging swing-something Ellen had always wanted.

Daniel hurried back to the hotel to get his wife and daughter. Both Ellen and Katie loved the house as he thought they would. The owners were eager to sell, so the sale went quickly. The two women worked quickly and were unpacked and settled into the house in just a few days. Daniel was pleased how quickly things were coming together.

Then, he began his next step. He started asking around about hiring a guide. According to the people at the general store, Trent, the mountain man, had not come to town yet. Daniel was too anxious to go and didn't want to sit around and wait, so he decided to find somebody else for the job. But he could find no one willing to go up into the Indian territory-except the old drunk in the saloon. Jed was willing to go for a bottle of cheap whiskey.

Daniel wasn't sure if the old man was telling the truth or not when he said he hunted and trapped all over the country and knew every inch of the trail. Furthermore, he said he could speak to most Indian tribes. *Maybe twenty years ago and sober he could,* Daniel thought. *But could he do it now?* Daniel wasn't even sure the old coot could walk a mile without collapsing. He'd have to think on this one awhile. Meanwhile, he would continue to look for someone capable of the job.

Three days later, Daniel and Jed started out. Daniel had made sure Jed left all the whiskey behind and promised to buy him a brand new bottle when they returned.

The first day went smoothly. Jed sang and laughed, unconcerned about the trail or direction they were headed. However, when Daniel awoke the next morning, Jed was a completely different person. When he found out what he had agreed to do, his face went white and his mouth gaped. Jed then proceeded to talk his way out of the mess he'd gotten himself in. "I did what?" asked Jed sharply.

"Jed, we made a deal and now you're backing out?"

"Naw, I ain't backing out!" spat Jed. He then resorted to yelling and cussing, stomping around and throwing things. "It's a waste of time. Them Injuns done kilt that girl by now."

"I'm going anyway," announced Daniel. "I've got to find out."

"You're a fool, tenderfoot. You're gonna get both us kilt," grumbled Jed. "But I guess I've done foolhardy things before."

Jed continued grumbling as they packed up their gear, got on their horses and rode off that morning. This time, Jed, now very sober, led the way and watched for danger. He proved true to his bragging in the saloon. He knew every trail, every clump of grass and where every gopher hole was or had been.

—◄◄◄│♪│▻▻▻—

Before sunrise, Standing Arrow and Trent left camp to follow the buffalo. A large group of warriors and a few of the women went with them. Knowing the main hunting party would be gone for a few days, Black Crow and his men disappeared like ghosts. They also were on a hunting trip, but not for food.

They rode south hoping to find wagons of white people or lone braves to destroy. Destruction and ruin obsessed them as they pushed on at a fast pace to cover the ground between them and innocent victims.

The hunting party rode steadily for half a day before sighting the contented beasts grazing in the valley. They hadn't moved far from where Trent had spotted them the day before. Devising a plan of attack, the warriors spread out, staying down wind of the hairy animals. Moving closer, the hunters closed in on the herd.

Standing Arrow gave the signal and each warrior's arrow soared through the air simultaneously, taking the beasts by surprise. Most of the arrows struck vital organs and the animals dropped to the ground. Other arrows that did not kill the beasts, angered them instead, and the herd began to stampede.

With a scream of "Yip, yip, yipee," the warriors were off on the chase, thundering down the valley and across the rolling hills. Each warrior hung low, riding as though he and his horse were one. They continued shooting arrows at the wild torrent of buffalo until they were satisfied they had enough meat for all.

As the warriors turned back, they saw the valley littered with buffalo carcasses. They were exhilarated. It had been a good hunt. The Cheyenne village would not be hungry through the long winter. Now that the animals had been brought down and the hunt was over, the women poured over the ridge onto the battlefield. They started skinning and butchering the steaming bodies while the warriors hurrahed and pranced around.

Since they were far from the village and there was much work to do, the warriors helped skin and butcher the kill. But it was up to the women to dry the meat and scrape the hides. Before nightfall the carcasses were skinned and all the meat was cut from the bones. The talk around the fire went late as each warrior gorged himself on fresh meat while telling his view of the hunt.

Standing Arrow did not speak to Elizabeth or acknowledge that she was there. By nightfall she had begun to worry she had pushed him too far, and that he was truly angry with her. She would work hard. Maybe that would make up for what she had done. Proud jovial warriors slept contently around the crackling fires, dreaming of this and other great hunts. They enjoyed visions of racing down the valleys with buffalo thundering around them, daringly hanging off their horses, letting arrows fly into the shaggy beasts and dodging safely away as the buffalo crumpled into the dust.

———◆———

Two wagons, unmoving and seemingly deserted, stood lonely on the vast prairie. Black Crow and his hunting party watched from the ridge for many hours. They detected no movement or life except for the mules that had probably been used to pull the wagons. The warriors were after scalps and had decided there were none here to be had. But then a woman appeared at the side of one of the wagons. She struggled to dip water from a barrel while holding herself upright against the wagon. When she completed the task, she slowly made her way back inside the wagon.

Without a second thought, the warriors attacked the two lone wagons. They circled the wagons, firing arrows at them as they raced around and around. When there was no evidence of resistance, Black Crow decided the woman must be alone. *This will be an easy scalp,* he thought.

As they entered the wagons, the braves found sick men, women and children in each wagon. Unconcerned about what the sickness might be, the braves brutally killed the men and children. They took seven scalps and dragged two feverish women along as captives.

Leaving their raid behind, the warriors traveled north to head back to the village. They would have to hurry to be back before Standing Arrow and his hunting party. When the warriors made camp that night, they tortured the women before scalping and killing them. In the morning, the warriors mounted their horses and rode off, leaving the mangled bloody bodies of the women lying where they had left them the night before.

Elizabeth had worked hard, harder than she had ever imagined she could. She was tired and ready to get some rest.

Pulling her blanket closer around her shoulders, she realized that in her haste to sneak off with the hunting party she had forgotten to bring a buffalo robe to keep her warm.

Elizabeth sat watching, half amused at the goings on around the campfire, and listening to the stories that the braves told with such enthusiasm. She noticed Standing Arrow and Trent off to one side. It seemed like they were having a discussion, and were both getting angry. She tried to make out their words, but they were too far away for her to hear more than a few words here and there. She thought they might be arguing over her since Trent said something about it not being proper. She could tell that Standing Arrow had came back with an angry retort, but she hadn't heard his words. Trent shrugged his shoulders. Standing Arrow turned and strode away with quick powerful strides.

Elizabeth decided she'd better stay clear of the chief. She didn't want to anger him further. Elizabeth rolled up in the thin blanket she had and prepared to sleep, figuring she was so tired that the coldness probably wouldn't bother her much.

She was about to drift off when Standing Arrow covered her with his buffalo robe and crawled in beside her. She was thankful for the extra warmth, but was not sure about having Standing Arrow that close to her. She pretended to be asleep and soon heard the steady breathing of Standing Arrow next to her.

Waking first, Standing Arrow silently knelt at Trent's side, gently touching his shoulder to awaken him but not to startle him. Opening his eyes instantly, Trent was prepared for any situation. Seeing Standing Arrow, Trent knew he was in no danger.

Rising, the two men traveled deeper into the woods, looking for something to hunt. A cougar or a bear would be their first choice. Either pelt would add nicely to their supply of plews.

Every year, Trent took hides into town for Standing Arrow and traded goods that would be of use to the Cheyenne. The women especially enjoyed the needles, awls and colorful beads. Trent brought back a limited supply of blankets and cloth each year. Mostly, he traded the Cheyenne pelts for axes and knives. Sometime, Trent would have the blacksmith fashion long spearheads for hunting buffalo and bring them to Standing Arrow.

Trent was worried that soon the young chief would be asking for *firesticks* for his warriors. He knew it wouldn't be long before all the Indian tribes had guns. There was enough war among the tribes as it was, but when guns were readily available to them, they might wipe each other out. Attacks on wagon trains and homesteaders would increase. Destruction and terror would reach out their ugly fingers and penetrate deeply into the vast western territories leaving no one-Indian or white-safe from sudden unexpected attacks that were deadly.

Trent also knew that if the Cheyenne didn't have rifles, they wouldn't be able to protect themselves and would eventually be wiped out by enemy tribes that did. He knew the time would come when he would have to teach Standing

Arrow and his braves about the *firesticks*. But for now he would say nothing until Standing Arrow asked.

Standing Arrow and Trent proceeded through the forest soundlessly, keeping their eyes and ears alert for any hint of movement or sound that would indicate wildlife close by. Both men heard the low guttural growl at the same instant. Whirling around as though they were one, they stood side by side staring up at an enormous grizzly bear. The bear—just twenty feet away—stood on its hind legs. He swung his massive deadly paws, tossed his head and growled angrily. Both men knew that with one swipe of a paw, the claws would easily shred a man. Each knew the danger they were in and each one faced it bravely. To run would mean certain death since a lumbering grizzly bear could easily catch a man. They must kill the bear—or be killed.

Standing Arrow notched an arrow while Trent poured powder into the pan of his flintlock. They must aim carefully since a wounded bear was by far more dangerous. Trent would most likely get only one shot at the giant grizzly. Being as close to the bear as he was, he would not have time to reload and would have to use his knife to finish off the bear if the shot did not kill him.

Standing Arrow released his arrow with a powerful force that embedded the arrow deeply into the heart of the beast. Only seconds later, the flintlock bellowed spouting fire and smoke as it ejected the lead ball into the head of the huge bear. Trent feverishly worked on reloading his flintlock while the bear angrily lunged forward, after being only momentarily stunned by the attack. Standing Arrow shouted a warning to Trent, but the bear was on him before he could reach safety. Standing Arrow let another arrow fly and quickly retreated.

Dropping onto all four feet, the bear enveloped Trent while Standing Arrow's arrow flew harmlessly over his head. Trent pulled out his knife just as the bear closed in on him. He fought desperately, plunging his knife in the bear's midsection repeatedly. Standing Arrow filled the bear with arrows as it slowly fell over the top of Trent, crushing him beneath his weight.

As the life drained from the bear, Standing Arrow faced yet another problem. Without his horse, he would have a hard time getting the mighty grizzly off his friend. Trent, still conscious and seemingly with no broken bones, was glad for Standing Arrow's help as he began the laborious struggle to free himself from the massive weight on top of him.

With that task completed, Standing Arrow made a thorough check of Trent's wounds. The bear apparently had been dying and had expended most of its strength by the time it had reached Trent. The wounds were superficial. He would be sore and stiff, but he should heal without complications.

They made short work of skinning the bear and saving choice cuts of meat. The trek back to camp was slow. Already exhausted from the fight with the bear, they were now burdened down with the hide and meat. Their spirits were high. It had been a good hunt.

The two friends entered the hunting camp just as the other warriors were rising from the short night's sleep. Fires happily crackled to life as the women began cutting meat into strips to be dried. Standing Arrow and Trent told of their hunt, leaving no details for the imagination to build on. Every move was retold in great detail. The younger warriors, awed by the telling, hung on every word. Their story ended with Trent showing where the powerful claws had raked across his back, leaving streaks of dried blood down his back.

Three of the warriors returned to the site and brought back the rest of the bear meat and other things Trent and Standing Arrow had left behind. The fat on the bear was very useful and much needed. Teeth and claws were used for ornamental purposes. Trent would be expected to make a necklace of the claws that nearly cost him his life.

The next day was much like the first. The women worked tirelessly, cutting strips of meat, scraping hides and doing various jobs to preserve all parts of the buffalo. Elizabeth labored beside the hard-working Cheyenne women for three days. Each night, Standing Arrow would put his buffalo robe over Elizabeth, who pretended to be asleep as he lay beside her.

Because the women now thought Elizabeth was the chief's woman, she sensed a new respect from them. A few even nodded or spoke to her. By the time the women had completed their task, the warriors had fashioned a travois to be pulled behind each horse. Hides, meat and useful bones were loaded on each travois as the journey home began.

Standing Arrow walked beside Elizabeth, but did not speak. Determined not to anger him further, Elizabeth also held her tongue. By mid-afternoon, Standing Arrow broke the silence.

"You work hard!" he stated flatly.

"Thank you," replied Elizabeth happily.

She knew this was a great compliment coming from the chief, but her thoughts were cut short when Standing Arrow continued brusquely. "You disobey. It is a bad thing to disobey the chief."

Elizabeth hung her head, knowing he was right. But at the same time she did not regret it. She had learned much, made new friends and had enjoyed the time working. Elizabeth prayed silently, asking God to give her the right words to say to the angry chief.

"Standing Arrow," she pleaded, "I know I should not have disobeyed, but I feel much safer with you than alone at the village. Little Robin does not like me and I have no friends there. You, Nakoma and Yellow Flower are my only friends, and you all were going to be on the hunt. I worked hard, and because of that I made some new friends. And who would have protected me from Black Crow and Snake at the village?"

She left the question unanswered, allowing Standing Arrow think it through on his own.

Later in the day, Standing Arrow spoke. "Sometimes a chief does not always make right decisions. You were wise in coming on hunt."

Elizabeth sighed with relief, knowing Standing Arrow was no longer angry with her.

"But the women on the hunt showed you respect because they think you are my wife," said Standing Arrow with a twinkle in his eye.

Elizabeth turned her horrified blue eyes to meet the amused gaze of the chief. "Why would they think that?" she demanded.

The amusement left Standing Arrow's face when he saw Elizabeth's response. "We shared the same buffalo robe at night."

Elizabeth remembered the argument she had heard Trent and Standing Arrow have that first night. The bits and pieces of the conversation were plain to her now. They had been arguing about who would share his robe with her.

She suddenly realized the impact of the whole situation and was secretly glad it had been Standing Arrow, but was sorry about the appearance of evil. "I am sorry if I have caused you problems among the people," she said softly.

Standing Arrow chuckled, and the twinkle returned as quickly as it had left.

The journey home was long and tiresome. All of the horses were burdened with heavy loads, and women and warriors walked methodically beside them. Standing Arrow was anxious to get back to the village and pushed the small group steadily on, stopping only once to allow the horses to rest.

Sitting together in the cool grass, Standing Arrow told Elizabeth why he was in such a hurry to get back. "The village has been left unprotected too long. The Commanche are like a hornet's nest. Something stirs them up. It is not good to be away." Standing Arrow's English had improved since Elizabeth had been there, and he spoke with her openly now.

Elizabeth continued to walk beside Standing Arrow when they resumed their journey. The closer they came to the village, the more wary the little group was. Standing Arrow stopped several times and, to Elizabeth's surprise, he effortlessly imitated an eagle call. She had heard this before but never knew it was Standing Arrow. He remained silent for a few minutes to listen and then motioned the group on. Elizabeth was puzzled, but decided to wait for an explanation.

Living in the Indian village Elizabeth had learned to listen and watch to learn. A short time later he repeated the call and then again later. Elizabeth finally understood when she heard a bobwhite answer his call. Shortly a bronze brave appeared, seemingly out of nowhere. Two Feathers met up with Standing Arrow, excited to tell the chief of the happenings in the village while he was away.

Elizabeth slowed her pace and merged with the other women in the group while Two Feathers told Standing Arrow that Black Crow and Snake had been the cause of the Commanche war parties. The chief knew he would have to deal harshly with them in order to save the Cheyenne people from a full war with the Commanche. In fact, he might have to turn Black Crow, Snake and a few other men over to the angry tribe. The Commanche chief would no doubt accept the trade for the lives of the dead. They would then torture the Cheyenne renegades to a slow death. That would satisfy the tribe and they would leave the Cheyenne village alone.

Chapter Seven

Daniel and Jed came upon the wagons in the mid-afternoon. It wasn't hard to read the signs. Even Daniel, who had lived most of his life in the city, could understand what had happened. The only sound that could be heard as the men silently dug graves for the mutilated bodies of the men and children was the scraping of the shovels and an occasional fly buzzing by.

Daniel had hoped they would find Elizabeth and the other women alive in the village. That hope was faint, and he had to keep reminding himself that he believed Elizabeth was alive. He was a stubborn man and he kept that flame of hope flickering.

Jed, on the other hand, was sure beyond a shadow of doubt that Elizabeth and the two women who had been taken from the wagons were all dead. He was just going because of the hope that Daniel carried. Jed didn't have anything better to do. He was eating good, breathing fresh air and . . . well, if he didn't make it back—he *was* getting old—he would rather die out here than in a smelly old room in town with cheap whiskey bottles around him.

Daniel and Jed pushed on past the wagons and made camp farther down the trail. Building a small fire, the two men ate out of necessity rather than enjoyment. Jed insisted that the fire had to be put out as soon as the coffee was hot and the food cooked. "We don't want them Injuns to see the fire and come after our scalps!"

That was all it took to get Jed started. Daniel wondered if the grizzled old man would talk all night. He told of his younger days, of trapping, fighting Indians and panning for gold. Daniel figured most of the stories were yarns. A few might have actually happened-parts of them, at least. All in all, Jed was a good storyteller and that's all that mattered. It kept their minds from wandering back to the scene they had just left.

They had managed to find addresses among the looted wagons and planned to notify relatives back East. The two men hoped to have a better day the next day.

Had they known what was ahead, they would not have altered their course, but they would have been better prepared to face the gruesome sight before them as they found where the Indians had camped after looting the wagons. Daniel quickly dismounted, taking only a few short steps and then retching violently.

Even Jed had believed the Indians would take the white women to the village and use them for slaves. He was troubled by the violence shown by these Indians.

He didn't believe they were Cheyenne or even Commanche—and Apache rarely came this far north. Were they renegades?

The two men worked side by side, silently giving the unfortunate women a proper burial. They would leave the details out when they notified the families of the victims.

Daniel prayed that Elizabeth had not had to go through the torment these women had. He was now sure she was dead. His goal changed as he shoveled dirt into the graves. He would follow these Indians, capture them and kill them. A long slow death.

Then he remembered the scripture that said, *"Vengeance is mine, saith the Lord."* Daniel wrestled with the problem, wanting to give these savages what they deserved, but in the end he knew he must let the Lord take care of the problem. Killing them was one thing, but torture was another.

Daniel and Jed continued on. Jed wanted to visit the Cheyenne chief since they were almost there. He hadn't been to their village for years. The chief was old the last time he had visited. Maybe he was dead and now a new younger chief was in charge. He would also ask if they knew who was spreading terror across the plains. Jed had seen Cheyenne arrows in the wagons but could not bring himself to believe the Cheyenne were capable of such ghastly deeds.

Black Crow pushed his small group on, wanting to get back before Standing Arrow arrived. But he was easily detoured if they came upon a lone warrior or a small defenseless group of people. Black Crow was ruthless. He killed and mutilated Indians and white alike. Proud of his deeds, he never tried to cover up or hide the evidence that pointed to the Cheyenne.

Black Crow was full of hate. He had been the chief of the dog soldiers when old Chief Lone Wolf had died. Black Crow thought he, instead of Standing Arrow, should have been made chief over all the people. But the people had made the right choice. Standing Arrow was a good chief and did what was best for the survival of the people.

Black Crow, on the other hand, would have killed the tribe off by now. He would have sent them into battles against the Commanche or Kiowas, starting unnecessary wars. Black Crow was a good chief of the dog soldiers. When given permission by the tribal chief, he had led his men into deadly battles where they were victorious. He thought what he was doing now would force the tribes to fight, and then the people would all turn to him. He didn't think about all the women and children of the Cheyenne tribe who would be killed or suffer. He was selfish and let his anger control his actions.

The hunting party returned before Black Crow and his men. Standing Arrow had already decided to punish Black Crow as soon as he arrived. The council would have to meet and decide what was to be done.

Black Crow made his return in the middle of the night, hoping Standing Arrow had not noticed his absence the day before. Each warrior that rode with Black Crow slept late in an effort to avoid a confrontation with the angry chief. The wives of the renegades had missed their husbands and were glad to let them stay in the lodge most of the day.

Deciding to wait no longer, Standing Arrow strode to Black Crow's lodge demanding to know what they had been doing and why they had fresh scalps. Black Crow shrugged unconcerned. "We were attacked."

Standing Arrow knew this to be a lie that Black Crow used every time, and every time none of the braves riding with him had battle wounds. Standing Arrow's anger rose as he tried to reason with the renegades. "You are causing the other tribes to make war on the Cheyenne. Women and children will die because of these deeds you have done."

Throwing his head back with a loud laugh, Black Crow suddenly sobered. "The people will follow me to war rather than run like women and children."

"Why should we make war when there is no reason?" asked Standing Arrow sternly.

"They are our enemy; we should destroy them," replied Black Crow angrily.

"If we do not bother them, they don't bother us," snapped the young chief.

"*I* should be chief." Black Crow pounded his protruding chest. "I would not run and hide from the enemy."

"We will not run and hide. We will face what you have brought on the tribe, but *you* will be punished," Standing Arrow replied dryly. Turning abruptly, Standing Arrow headed for his own lodge.

Trent and Elizabeth were at the fire discussing their journey to Julesburg. Already in a black mood, Standing Arrow left the lodge and took refuge at the stream. The tranquillity he found was short-lived. A commotion in the center of the village brought him quickly to his feet and on his way back to camp.

Black Crow was strutting through camp, displaying the scalps he and his men had taken. "Many Scalps," Black Crow said enticingly, shaking the pole that the scalps hung from. "Many scalps could hang from our lodges. We must fight all our enemies." Proudly he taunted the people. "We must not run and hide like scared rabbit."

For the most part, the dog soldiers were loyal to Standing Arrow as their chief. Standing Arrow knew who the few were that rode with Black Crow out of loyalty and which ones went with him only because he was the chief of the dog soldiers.

The people milled around, watching with amusement. Black Crow continued his charade in an effort to divide the people and fill their heads with uncertainty.

Standing Arrow approached Black Crow. Facing him, he told the people how Black Crow had raided and killed only lone braves, woman and children, and the elderly, sick and crippled. He had never fought a battle against strong warriors. Looking at the people, Standing Arrow continued to tell them that if Black Crow were chief, the tribe would be no more. He would lead them all to an early death.

Black Crow, realizing only a small number of the people were showing loyalty to him, was angry. He spat on the ground in front of Standing Arrow and stalked away in a rage. Standing Arrow's mood only worsened as the night drew on.

Elizabeth really didn't have much preparation to make as she got ready to leave. There were only a few friends she wanted to say good-bye to. Yellow Flower and Elizabeth spent most of the evening together. They talked, laughed and even cried.

Later, Elizabeth sat by the stream hoping Standing Arrow would come. It was a beautiful night. The stars winked down, the air was crisp but not cold, and as the sun slipped behind the mountains, the hills were showered with an array of reds and yellows. She reluctantly returned to the lodge to a night of restlessness.

Elizabeth, Standing Arrow and Trent were up before dawn broke. Standing Arrow helped Trent load the pelts onto three packhorses. She assured Standing Arrow she could lead a packhorse. Trent would have to lead the other two. Elizabeth was pleased to be able to do this final thing for the Cheyenne. These were their pelts and they needed items from the whites. She would help Trent purchase supplies for them. She was determined to find something special for Yellow Flower.

"Good-bye, Standing Arrow," Elizabeth said softly. "Thank you for caring for me while I was here, and letting me stay in your lodge."

The young chief stood solemnly before her. He didn't speak a word. The lines of his face were hard and cold as granite. Elizabeth's heart ached for him. Even when he was unhappy, she thought he was quite handsome. His broad shoulders seemed to droop a little, but he still stood proud. She wanted to hug him good-bye but decided against it.

"Good-bye," she repeated as she quickly mounted.

Elizabeth nodded to Trent and they started off.

The tears flowed freely when the Cheyenne village was no longer in sight. She had an uneasy feeling about leaving. Was it because she would miss them? Or was it because danger lurked ahead? Elizabeth knew Standing Arrow would not let Black Crow and his men leave the village until she had had a chance to reach safety. He was still taking care of her. She wished now that she would have hugged Standing Arrow. It was not their custom for unmarried men and women to hug, but he would have understood.

Her thoughts were then broken by a long shrill eagle call, causing her horse to draw to a stop. Elizabeth instinctively looked to the sky for an eagle flying overhead. But she knew it had been Standing Arrow. That was his final good-bye. Turning, she looked back and scanned the hills, but he was nowhere to be seen.

The Commanche were looking for revenge—and they didn't seem to care who they took it on. They would be careful not to kill their victims. It would be more rewarding to take them to camp for a slow death. The whole tribe would want to share in the revenge.

When the two white men rode into the ravine, they had little chance against the angry Indians. Even Jed hadn't suspected the attack. The only warning Jed had was a brief swooshing noise. The war club hit him in the back of the head, flipping him over the head of his mustang. Jed didn't feel the jolt of the fall because he was already unconscious when he hit the ground.

Daniel was in a similar situation, only he was still conscious when his body slammed into the dirt. As he rolled quickly to get his feet under him, another blow from a flying war club sent him sprawling out cold.

When they awoke, they found themselves draped over their horses and tied securely. Daniel's feet and hands were already numb. His head hung low at the horse's sides and pounded with pain. Daniel wasn't sure if the pain was from the blood running to his head or from the club that had knocked him to the ground. Turning his head slightly, He could see Jed was in the same painful position as he was. *At least I'm alive,* Daniel thought.

The Commanche rode several long hours before coming to their village where the warriors were greeted with a loud cheerful reception. Jed could speak a little Commanche and understood most. He gathered that this group was the first to return with captives, that two more war parties were still out. Daniel and Jed were deposited roughly into a tepee. Each man had his hands and feet bound tightly with rawhide straps. The door was shut and a guard posted. They would be kept there until more captives were brought in.

Elizabeth rode silently most of the day. She should be happy she was returning to a town, but somehow the joy wasn't there. She began to imagine her return. First, she must wire her family in the East and then she must buy a new dress. Her deerskin dress would never do in town. Fingering its soft folds, she realized how beautiful and yet simple and comfortable it was. She would always keep the dress to remember her time with the Cheyenne.

Her thoughts of a tall muscular Cheyenne chief wearing fringed leggings and a breech clout that was ornately decorated with porcupine quills down the length of the legs startled her. Drawing a sharp breath, she willed her thoughts to move on.

She had very little money. Three twenty-dollar gold pieces seemed a large sum, but when she thought about having to pay for a room at the hotel, new clothes and food, she knew it wouldn't last long. She would have to find a job as soon as she possibly could.

A heaviness settled over her. *Why can't the whites live simply, like the Cheyenne?* she wondered. Life was so carefree and simple at the village. It's not that the Cheyenne didn't have work-hard work—to do. And they always had to think about protecting the village. But so did the whites. *What was the difference?* Elizabeth pondered this thought for a long while without coming to a conclusion.

Trent stopped at a stream to let the horses drink and rest awhile. Not knowing what to say to Elizabeth, he kept silent. He never knew what to say to women. Elizabeth was one of the prettiest girls he had ever laid his eyes on, but he kept to himself and didn't see many women. It would be nice to have a woman like Elizabeth. She had already adapted to life with the Cheyenne. Maybe he would ask her to come back to the mountains with him after she wired her folks. The sound of Elizabeth's voice startled him out of deep thought. "What?" he asked. "I'm sorry—I didn't hear you."

Repeating herself, Elizabeth asked, "Why is life out here with the Indians so tranquil?"

Trent looked into the innocent blue eyes of a young lady who had not had to face the truth of life yet. How could he tell her the whites were greedy, slothful and selfish? He had never heard of an Indian making another Indian pay to sleep in his lodge or to feed a visitor passing through. True, Indians traded things among themselves, but that was out of respect and wasn't considered as payment. Shaking his head, he answered, "I don't know for sure. Maybe it's just the difference in attitude."

"Attitude?"

Twisting the long fringe on his buckskin shirt, Trent sighed. "Yes ma'am. I think that's a big part of it."

She wasn't sure what he meant by that answer. How were their attitudes different? She would have to think about that for awhile.

"We better mount up," he said as he walked toward the horses. Gathering the reins, he turned to see if Elizabeth was ready. She just stood there, staring with a lonely empty look toward the Cheyenne village. Then she looked to the sky, hoping to see an eagle or hear the unmistakable eagle cry belonging to Standing Arrow. He knew her heart belonged with Standing Arrow. He felt a sadness for both of them. What was so important to her that she had to go back? She had just said life was tranquil with the Cheyenne. "Ma'am are you sure you want to go back?" he asked.

Jerked from her stupor, Elizabeth replied hastily, "Why . . . yes. What ever made you think I didn't?"

"Ma'am I'm no judge of love by any means, but that look in your eyes betrays your feelings easy enough!"

"Please, my name is Elizabeth, and I think you are seeing things," she replied curtly.

"Yes ma'am . . . maybe I am," replied Trent quietly.

Elizabeth mounted up, still in a huff over what Trent had said. He was crazy if he thought she loved Standing Arrow.

They hadn't traveled far when Trent pulled up and motioned for her to keep quiet. They sat on their horses and listened carefully, but didn't hear a sound. Not even the birds were making noise. Trent knew danger was near. The birds' silence meant only one thing—something was close by that scared them away. It was too quiet—an eerie quiet. Trent scanned the trees and ravine but saw nothing.

Out of nowhere, six Commanche braves suddenly were yipping and yelling as they rode thundering horses toward them. Letting the pack animals go, Trent grabbed the bridle of Elizabeth's horse, turning it and slapping a wicked blow to its rump.

"Ride" he yelled. "Ride as fast as you can."

Elizabeth's horse leaped, almost unseating her. The Commanche were slowly gaining on them, but Trent and Elizabeth's horses were both hardy, well-bred mustangs who kept up the pace. An arrow flew past her head and at the same instant Trent fell forward over his horse's neck. Elizabeth could see the arrow protruding from his left shoulder. Blood was already staining his shirt. Fear grabbed at her heart. She knew they wouldn't get away.

Trent tumbled from the horse and landed in a crumpled heap. At the same time something hard hit Elizabeth in the back of the head. She started to fall and then all went black.

When she regained consciousness, she found herself slung over a pony's back in front of a large, smelly warrior. She squirmed a little, trying to ease some of the pain. The warrior pushed down hard on the middle of her back. Elizabeth figured out quickly that it was best to be still no matter the discomfort.

When they reached the Commanche village, she was roughly pushed to the ground and the warriors taunted her, poking her with sticks and trying to touch her blonde hair. They were trying to make her beg for her life or cry out.

Thinking they might know some of the Cheyenne language, she spoke loud hissing the words for all to hear. "I will not beg for my life no matter what torture you use. I will die brave and proud like the Cheyenne!"

The braves laughed and shoved her to a tepee and pushed her inside. As soon as her eyes adjusted to the darkness she could tell she was alone. Dropping to the ground in exhaustion, she prayed that Trent was not dead. They didn't bring him to camp, so Elizabeth assumed the worst.

Chapter Eight

With hands and feet numb from the rawhide that bound them, Daniel began to wonder if he was indeed a fool for coming out to this raw land on a search that was impossible. For the first time he realized that if he were killed, Ellen and Katie would be on their own. *What a fool I've been,* Daniel thought. *I've risked the whole family over one that is most likely dead.* But that uncertainty was something he wasn't sure he could live with. Daniel thought about Jesus leaving the ninety-and-nine to go after the one. That scripture brought comfort to him.

Jed grunted and tried to roll over.

"Jed . . . Jed, are you all right?"

"No I ain't all right. Do I look all right? I'm in a te-pee, tied up with my face smashed in the dirt an' I'm sure them thar redskins ain't gonna rub my sore back when they come back!"

"Jed, I'm sorry. This is my fault. You were right. This was a fool thing to do. If we can escape, I'm ready to go home," Daniel stated solemnly. He was not feeling sorry for himself nor was he afraid to die. He merely was facing reality.

Their thoughts were interrupted by a commotion outside. A second war party had apparently returned. They heard a woman speaking in a loud hateful voice.

"Jed, what's she saying?" asked Daniel.

Shaking his head he answered. "They've captured a Cheyenne woman. She's telling them she will not scream for mercy if they torture her."

Puzzled, Daniel listened to the woman. It sounded like his dear Elizabeth's voice, only in another language. Daniel shook the feeling away by telling himself he was just imagining it.

Trent was wise in the ways of survival in the plains. He knew they couldn't escape, and he also knew he must save Elizabeth. When the arrow struck his shoulder, he decided to make his move. He tumbled from the horse and landed in such a way that the Indians assumed him dead. He hoped they were in a hurry and would not come after his scalp. If they did, he would have to be ready to use his knife.

He remained very still and breathed very lightly. It didn't take long for them to capture Elizabeth and ride away. In his heart he prayed he could get help before they hurt her. He hadn't been much on prayer lately, but his mama had taught him about prayer when he was a youngster. And right now, that was all the help he could offer Elizabeth. He saw her fall from her horse and knew she would be unconscious most of the way to the Commanche village.

Easing himself to a sitting position, Trent explored the wound with his right hand and found that the arrow had been a long shot and had not embedded itself too deeply. He would be sore for awhile, but it would heal. But removing the arrow proved to be more painful than he had expected. He sat back to rest and let his head clear. Regaining some strength, he began making his way back to the Cheyenne village. On foot it would take much longer. Trent whistled for his horse, but as he expected the horse had been scared and had run off. An hour later he picked up sign of the packhorses. They were headed back to the village.

Trent stumbled on, knowing each step brought him closer to help. With each step he also lost more blood. His back was now soaked with blood, and he could feel it running down his leg. The arrow must have gone deeper than he had thought. He must make it to camp. He must save Elizabeth. Weakened and exhausted, Trent fell to the ground unconscious.

Standing Arrow had been sulking about camp all day, barking out orders and commands to anyone who crossed his path. The wives of Black Crow, Snake and the other men who rode with Black Crow's raiding parties told Standing Arrow their husbands couldn't be disturbed because they were sick.

Standing Arrow thought it strange that they were all sick at the same time. They were up to something— and Standing Arrow didn't like it. He wanted to see them and make sure they were really in the village and not going after Trent and Elizabeth.

Striding angrily across camp to Black Crow's tepee, Standing Arrow spotted something coming over the hill. Stopping, he stared hard at the objects. Realizing what he was seeing, he ran to his horse and mounted in a flash, racing out of camp at a tremendous speed.

He caught up the bridles of the packhorses, Trent's black mare and Elizabeth's mount. Standing Arrow brought them back into the village. Dismounting, he checked Trent's mare first. When he found blood on the saddle, he acted quickly. He left Nakoma in charge and took two braves with him that he knew were willing to fight to the death.

Back-tracking the horses, Standing Arrow and the warriors found Trent at about sundown. He was still alive, but had lost a lot of blood. If they could get him back where he could be cared for, he might make it.

Trent revived long enough to tell Standing Arrow what had happened. The last thing he remembered before passing out again was the cold stony look on Standing Arrow's face and the eyes that seemed to have fire burning behind them.

Standing Arrow instructed one of the warriors to take Trent back to camp and the other to come with him. Wheeling their horses Standing Arrow and Two Birds raced toward the Commanche village. It would be dark when they reached their destination. Standing Arrow was pleased with that since he could sneak in a lot easier that way.

Tying their mounts at a safe distance from the village, they worked their way through the terrain on foot until they viewed the whole camp. Standing Arrow and Two Birds studied each lodge carefully until they both agreed there were only two lodges that could contain captives.

Ever so carefully, they inched their way to the nearest one. Standing Arrow quietly and slowly pulled two stakes out that were holding the edge of the tepee down. Moving slowly, he slithered under the edge and into the lodge while Two Birds kept watch.

It took a few minutes for his eyes to adjust inside the lodge, and then he saw two prone forms across from him. As he drew his knife, he crossed to the other side and knelt beside the forms. He saw that they were white men.

Jed woke with a start, but did not speak. Standing Arrow lost no time cutting him and Daniel loose and then disappeared into the darkness. Confused, Daniel whispered, "Why were we cut loose?"

"That thar Injun was a Cheyenne buck. He's a comin' after the Cheyenne woman. We'll watch, and wait until she's free 'fore we make a run fer it or they ain't got a chance of getting away. We gotta go out together, cuz no matter how quiet we are, them Commanche'll hear us."

Moving to the other side of the lodge, they lay on their bellies looking out under the edge of the lodge. They could just make out a figure lying at the back of the other captive lodge. They waited patiently.

Elizabeth was not sleeping and heard a faint sound. Listening carefully, she heard it again. All was quiet and then that faint sound again. Puzzled, she thought it sounded like wooden stakes being pulled up. Suddenly she sensed the presence of another person. Quickly rolling over and into a sitting position, she was happily surprised to see Standing Arrow coming under the side of the lodge. He motioned for her to stay very still and quiet. Elizabeth obeyed instantly. He cut her loose and both of them crawled back out under the buffalo hide cover in a matter of seconds.

Had she come out alone, Daniel would have seen her blonde hair and recognized his daughter. But Standing Arrow and Elizabeth came out together and his body blocked any view of Elizabeth that would identify her.

Elizabeth walked quietly to the edge of the trees, Standing Arrow and Two Birds directly behind her. Upon reaching the trees, the trio broke into a run. They covered the short distance to the horses rapidly. Standing Arrow mounted in one swift motion and reaching down, swung Elizabeth up behind him. They were off at a good pace.

Seeing that the three Indians had reached the cover of the trees safely, Jed and Daniel made their way out of the lodge carefully and into the trees. The Commanche never knew until morning that all three of their captives had escaped.

Elizabeth held onto Standing Arrow tightly for what seemed like hours as they made their getaway. When Standing Arrow and two Birds slowed their pace, Elizabeth relaxed and then began to be drowsy. Laying her head on Standing Arrow's broad back she fell asleep almost instantly.

The sun was just beginning to peak over the horizon when they rode into the Cheyenne village. It was a breathtaking sight to see the tepees with smoke lazily rolling out of the darkened tops silhouetted in the early dawn light. She was glad to be back, but she knew it would just mean another good-bye.

Before getting some sleep, Standing Arrow and Elizabeth checked on Trent. He was sleeping soundly. Yellow Flower reported he was regaining his strength fast, and would be fine in a few days.

Elizabeth saw concern in her friend's eyes. "Are you sure he's all right?"

"Yes, he's fine, but the others are not."

"Others?" repeated Elizabeth.

Looking at Standing Arrow, Yellow Flower answered. "Black Crow, Snake, Eagle Claw and Black Wing are very sick. Their bodies are hot with fever and they have red sores all over them."

As Yellow Flower described the illness Elizabeth's heart sank Trying to remain calm she demanded, "I must see one of them!"

"I'll take you to Snake's lodge," replied Yellow Flower.

"No," said Elizabeth, trying not to shout. "Stay away. I'll go alone."

Elizabeth was out of the lodge and on her way before anyone could argue. She reached Snake's lodge and called out to Beaver Woman to warn her before she entered. Beaver Woman had never liked Elizabeth, so she didn't wait for a response before going in. Kneeling by the feverish warrior, she needed only a quick look to confirm her fears.

Retracing her steps, she entered Yellow Flower's lodge. "Yellow Flower have you or Nakoma cared for any of these men?" demanded Elizabeth.

"Yes," replied Yellow Flower hesitantly. "Yesterday I went to Snake's lodge to help while Beaver Woman rested. She has cared for him for four days."

Turning to Standing Arrow, Elizabeth said, "You must tell all the people who have not been in the lodges of the sick to stay far away and to move higher up stream for drinking water."

Standing Arrow and Nakoma both rose to their feet warily. Standing Arrow voiced the question they all had: "And what of those who have?"

"They must stay away, but they must also stay away from the others!"

"Who will care for the sick?" questioned Yellow Flower.

"I will help the wives of those already sick and then when the wives and children are sick I will care for them," stated Elizabeth.

Unconvinced, Standing Arrow left the tepee with long powerful strides. He was almost to Black Crow's lodge when Elizabeth caught up to him. Standing in front of him, she put the palms of her hands on his massive chest.

"Stop," she cried. "Standing Arrow, stop! You musn't go in there." She could see he was angry, but she didn't care. She must make him understand.

"I am the chief. I must go see!"

"No please, you will die if you go in there."

"And what of you?" Standing Arrow asked.

Sighing, Elizabeth wasn't sure he would fully understand, but she must try to explain. "This is a bad disease. You must have medicine to get over it. I had it when I was a child."

"You didn't die," interrupted Standing Arrow.

"No, I didn't, but I had medicine and now I won't get it again."

"And Trent? He won't die from this disease either?" questioned Standing Arrow.

"I don't know," replied Elizabeth. "If he has already had it, he won't. But if not, he will die like the rest."

Standing Arrow was confused and scared for his people, so he decided to do what Elizabeth asked.

Black Crow's lodge was the biggest, so with the help of their wives, Snake, Eagle Claw and Black Wing were moved to Black Crow's lodge. The women then took turns sleeping, carrying water, caring for the children and bathing the feverish men.

Three days later Elizabeth noticed Beaver Woman was beginning to look feverish. Elizabeth motioned for her to lie down.

It was not long before the other three women and the children were also feverish. The children lay at their parents' sides. All had a raging fever, and ugly sores covered their bodies. Elizabeth now had seventeen sick Cheyenne in one lodge to care for. She directed most of her attention to the children, trying to keep them as comfortable as possible.

When the men started dying, Elizabeth was thankful that their wives and children were sick enough to not know what was happening. Elizabeth wasn't sorry for these men. They deserved to die, but she hated the fact that she knew they would go to the fiery pit of hell.

She prayed constantly while caring for the dying Cheyenne people. Every chance she got, she talked with the children and wives, telling them about Jesus and his love for them. She even tried to tell the men that had treated her so brutally. The children seemed willing to listen and a few gave their lives to Christ, but the men and women were stubborn and would not listen.

Elizabeth now faced another problem. What was she going to do with the bodies of the dead? Trent was the answer to that prayer. He had regained most of his strength and insisted on helping her. Poking his head into the sweaty lodge, he asked if he could help.

"Have you had smallpox?"

"Yes," he replied as he entered the lodge.

Elizabeth sighed. "I do need help," she said with a weary smile.

Still a little weak, Trent needed Elizabeth's help to carry the bodies out. In just two more days, several of the children had died as well as two of the women. By the next morning, six more people had come to the sick lodge burning up with fever.

"We need medicine, Trent. Most of the tribe will die without it," Elizabeth said desperately.

"Can you manage a few days without me?"

Surprised, Elizabeth searched his face. She knew what he was thinking! "Trent, are you strong enough? Do you really think you could make it?"

"Sure, I'll make it. I have to," he replied confidently. With that decision made, he scrambled to his feet and out of the lodge. Selecting two stout horses, he loaded them with pelts and caught up his black mare. From a distance, he told Standing Arrow what was happening and then slapped the reins across the mare's rump and was off.

He could make it to Julesburg in a day and a half if he didn't stop. He might kill the horses in doing so, but he would try to give them short rests. They were sound mares. *They'll make it*, he thought to himself. He really hated to give up his black mare, but he would have to have a fresh mount to make the trek back.

Chapter Nine

Jed and Daniel traveled at a fast pace most of the night. They were headed for Julesburg. Daniel was convinced Elizabeth was dead and he should go back to his wife and Katie.

Jed, on the other hand, wanted to go on to other tribes.

"We've lost our weapons and horses," Daniel argued. "We should go home while we still have our lives." In the end Daniel won and they headed south toward Julesburg.

Five days later, they stumbled into Julesburg tired and hungry. Ellen and Katie took the news hard.

"Are you sure, Papa?" cried Katie.

Daniel was not sure, but he had to force reassurance. "Yes, Katie dear. A white woman just doesn't survive with the Indians." He didn't tell her and Ellen the gruesome sights he and Jed had seen when they came upon white women who had been captured by the savages. It was bad enough that *he* had to think of his darling Elizabeth being tortured like that, but Ellen and Katie needn't know.

Ellen said little and simply busied herself with cooking and cleaning. She grieved silently.

Katie, on the other hand, threw herself across her bed and sobbed until there were no more tears left and sleep finally claimed her.

⁓∘⫸∘⫷∘⁓

Trent rode at a fast clip for hours. Every delay could mean another life. He must continue. He reached Julesburg at about three in the morning. Unloading the pack animals in front of the general store, he curried the tired mounts and turned them into the livery stables. Trent found a nice spot under a tree and slept soundly until morning. As soon as the owner opened the general store, Trent was there ready to sell the pelts. He got a good price for the majority of the furs and left the store pleased. His next stop was the doctor's office.

The doctor was reluctant at first, but because he knew Trent, he decided to help him out. The medicine took a large portion of the money he had gotten from the pelts; therefore, he would be limited on what he could buy at the general store. Stashing the medicine in his saddlebags, he then returned to the general store. While the storekeeper was gathering the items on his list, Trent looked around at the knives and guns.

Looking up as a young woman entered, Trent caught his breath. He could tell she was troubled, but even the sadness couldn't hide the beauty. She was undoubtedly the most beautiful woman he had ever seen. Katie, aware of Trent's gaze, spoke to him.

"Hello."

"I'm sorry, ma'am," stuttered Trent as he removed his hat. "I didn't mean to stare. It's just that you look so much like a friend of mine, you could be her sister."

Suddenly sobering, Katie replied heatedly, "I don't have a sister anymore."

"Anymore?" Trent asked, puzzled.

"The Indians captured her from the stage last spring," Katie stated with tears pooling in her large blue eyes.

"Elizabeth," whispered Trent. "You're Elizabeth's sister."

Hearing Elizabeth's name spoken, Katie instantly lost the ladylike demeanor she had been taught in the East. "Did you see Elizabeth?" she demanded loudly as she rushed to Trent's side.

"Yes ma'am," replied Trent, smiling broadly.

But before he could tell her that Elizabeth was alive, Katie grabbed the front of his shirt and began yanking on him, shaking him and screaming at him. "Where is she? Is she dead?"

Taken aback, Trent let her unleash her anger on his shirt for a minute. Then, reaching up, he took her hands from his shirt and held her still. Her anger subsided and Katie began to sob. Relaxing a little, Trent held her close briefly. Pushing her back at arm's length, Trent looked into her agonized eyes.

"Elizabeth Mayfield is alive. She's living in the Cheyenne village."

Katie's eyes flashed with hope as her lips formed a lopsided smile. "I knew she was alive. I could feel it. But Papa said when he got back from the Commanche village that she was dead. Please come tell Mama and Papa that Elizabeth is alive. Please."

Unable to refuse, Trent followed the young lady out of the store and down the street. Daniel and Ellen listened quietly while Trent told them what he knew of Elizabeth. "Why didn't she come back with you?" questioned Daniel.

"We started out two weeks ago. The Commanche captured Elizabeth and left me with an arrow in my shoulder. They were in a hurry, and didn't make sure I was dead. Standing Arrow rescued her and took her back to the Cheyenne village!"

Daniel pounded his fist sharply on the tabletop. "I heard her voice there. I was so close."

"You were there?" asked Trent.

"Yes, we were also captured and a tall powerful looking Cheyenne brave cut us loose," replied Daniel.

Trent knew instantly that it was Standing Arrow. "That was the chief of the Cheyenne."

"Elizabeth spoke the Cheyenne language when she was brought to the Commanche camp," Daniel added with wonder in his voice.

"Yes, she speaks it fluently."

"You never said why she didn't come with you."

"Smallpox has hit the village. Many have died, and most will die if I don't hurry back with medicine. Elizabeth has been caring for them for many days. She couldn't leave yet. I will bring her back as soon as the village is well," he added as he stood up.

After shaking hands with Daniel, Trent left. He stopped at the store to pick up his supplies and then to the livery to find a horse. The hostler at the livery assured Trent he would care for the black mare and promised not to sell it before Trent returned.

Trent picked a stocky bay mare and began saddling up just as Katie came through the doorway. Seeing Katie again startled Trent, and his stomach felt fluttery. *Why does this girl have such an affect on me?* he wondered.

"Trent, please, do you have room to take Elizabeth a letter?" questioned Katie.

"Yes, ma'am, I sure do."

"Thank you! Trent, I was wondering," Katie began slowly, "would you take me with you to the Indians' camp?"

"No." His reply was quick and very sharp.

"Why not?"

"It's dangerous."

"But Elizabeth's there," pleaded Katie.

"It's safe there!" Trent countered.

"You just said it was dangerous!" replied Katie bewildered.

Annoyed and anxious to be on the way and away from Katie, Trent spoke harshly. "The trip to camp is dangerous."

"So you won't take me?"

"No," replied Trent as he mounted the bay and left Katie standing in the doorway of the livery.

Humph, I'll show him, thought Katie.

"Get my horse saddled. I'll be back," she hollered to the hostler.

Katie made quick work of throwing a few supplies in her saddlebags, changed her clothes and left a note for her father. The thought of danger never crossed her mind as she mounted up and headed off after Trent.

She spotted him several times but kept a safe distance behind him. Had he not been in such a hurry and thinking about the woman with the large blue eyes, he would have noticed a rider following him.

Katie rode most of the day with thoughts of the tall young mountain man clad in fringed buckskin racing through her mind. The bright strips of decoration down the front of his shirt had intrigued her. What was it and who had done it? Did he have a wife? She remembered when she touched his shirt in the general store that the decoration had felt smooth but stiff. *I'll ask him, if I ever get close enough to catch up to him.* Katie kept up the pace all day and had finally decided it was time catch up to him when something knocked her from her horse.

She hit the ground hard, and the weight of something crashed down on top of her. Opening her eyes, she saw the uplifted hand with a long shiny knife coming down at her. Trent stopped suddenly when he realized it was Katie. He pushed her away roughly. "I could have killed you sneaking up on me like that."

Shaken and still in a huff, Katie replied, "I wasn't sneaking. Just following."

"I told you you couldn't come," growled Trent.

"You can't send me back now, not alone!" taunted Katie.

Trent's anger overruled the situation. Coming close to Katie's face, he hissed, "Be very quiet. There are Indian war parties lurking about looking for scalps-especially pretty blonde ones."

When he saw he had her full attention, he grabbed her up, flung her across his knees and paddled her soundly. Finishing the job, he roughly pushed her to the ground.

Katie had not uttered a sound throughout the whole ordeal. Quickly gathering her skirt and getting her feet under her, she rose in a fit of rage. "I'm still going with you," she spat quietly, keeping her face close to his so only he would hear. Turning, she marched off into the darkness.

Trent drew a long deep breath of the chilly night air and released it slowly. His body was still shaking with the realization that he had almost killed Katie. He was not in the habit of looking over a victim that came out of the darkness toward him in the heart of Indian country. It was some hidden instinct within him that made him pause briefly before plunging the knife down. He doubted she even realized how close she had came to death.

That same feeling he had at the livery stable began to creep into his stomach again. But this time he dismissed it with disgust. *Any man bound to that "she cat" would have a hard life. He would probably end up beating her to death.* Shaking those kind of thoughts about Katie from his mind, he prepared to head out.

They managed to leave quietly and with no disagreements. Traveling at a fast pace, the pair covered the open country rapidly. Digging in his saddlebags, Trent pulled out a large piece of jerky and handed it to Katie. "It's not much of a supper, but I'm sure it's more than you planned for!" remarked Trent sarcastically.

Katie took the jerky with a smile and began chewing and tugging on the strip of meat like Trent did. Laughing softly to herself, Katie thought this sure wasn't a ladylike food to eat. The jerky was good and lasted a long time. It also kept her mind off the long ride.

Eventually Trent felt more at ease with Katie and began talking to her, telling her about his trapping camp and how to live off the land. He was actually enjoying their time together. He had never been able to talk to a girl like he was talking with Katie—not even Elizabeth.

"Do you really know the chief of the Cheyenne Indians?" asked Katie doubtfully.

"Yes, we hunt together," replied Trent, smiling boyishly.

"And Elizabeth actually lives there with them?"

Chuckling, Trent replied, "Elizabeth lives in the lodge of the chief."

"Really?"

The darkness had closed in around them hours ago, but Trent kept them at a relentless pace. Katie knew Trent must be getting hungry-men were always hungry. She pulled two sandwiches with thick slices of ham in them from her saddlebags. With an impish grin, she offered one to Trent. "It isn't a home-cooked meal, but I guess it will do in a pinch."

Trent, chuckling softly, took the sandwich and thanked her. Katie, knowing she had won that round, laughed gaily.

As the gray of pre-dawn disappeared, the horizon displayed an array of colors. Trent had them traveling slower now, and he seemed more wary. He knew he would have to be extremely careful. If he weren't, it would cost them their lives and the lives of the Cheyenne tribe. With his trained eye, he continuously scanned the hills and valleys.

Swiftly dismounting, Trent pulled Katie down and instructed her to stay quiet and very close to him. They led the horses into a thick stand of cottonwood trees growing in groves along the valley's edge. Peering through the leaves, they watched a war party of Commanche trot by at an uncomfortably close distance.

Katie's heart beat rapidly, but it wasn't from fear. She felt safe with this rugged mountain man—but she had never seen Indians before.

Trent's heart was also racing. He knew that if the Indians found them, they wouldn't have a chance. He was still weak from the last Commanche attack. The wound was healing nicely, but it would still be a while before he was ready to fight off several Indians at a time in hand-to-hand combat.

The painted braves rode on steadily and didn't look back. Looking at Katie, Trent sighed. "That was a little too close for comfort. We better stay here for a little while to make sure they're gone." While he watered and picketed the horses, Katie found some biscuits and cheese in her saddlebags.

Hidden among the trees, they sat in the lush grass and ate breakfast. The biscuits were good even if they were cold.

Taking their time and needing the rest, they nibbled slowly on the food and savored each bite. Trent talked about the Cheyenne encampment, trying to prepare Katie for their arrival.

"I just can't imagine Elizabeth living in a tepee," exclaimed Katie. "And speaking their language."

Trent smiled as she chattered on. He knew nothing he could tell her would prepare her for the reunion with Elizabeth.

Chapter Ten

Elizabeth awoke with a start. Her body screamed with fatigue and her head pounded. Looking around, it took a minute for her to realize where she was. She had been exhausted and had fallen asleep holding an infant. The cry of another child brought her back to her senses.

Putting the lifeless baby down, she scrambled to her feet and made her way to the ailing child. Elizabeth bathed the little girl and gave her a drink before surveying the rest of the bodies. Three more had died in the night.

Hearing a familiar noise outside, Elizabeth knew she would have to make room for more. It was already crowded in the lodge and she barely had room to walk among her charges. Elizabeth opened the door, hoping the newcomers were not too sick to help her remove the dead. She was not prepared for the eyes that met hers.

Nakoma and Yellow Flower stood at the door, each holding the other one up. Both were haggard and feverish.

Looking beyond them, her heart was suddenly in her throat. Elizabeth saw Standing Arrow staggering up the path as he carried Little Robin. Elizabeth didn't know if she could bear to watch her dearest friends suffer and die. Standing Arrow was so big and powerfully strong. To see him weak and helpless was more than she could take.

Dear Lord, please help me to make it through this. I can't do it by myself. Please watch over Trent and bring him back with medicine before more die. Help me, Lord, to bring the sick to the saving knowledge of your Son Jesus Christ. I know you love these people and want them to go to heaven. Use me to show them the way. Romans 8:28 says that "all things work together for good to them that love God, to them who are the called according to his purpose." Lord, I'm honored you chose me. My purpose was to come here to tell these people about you. Help me to be strong and face each trial. In Jesus name, Amen.

After her prayer, Elizabeth made a decision. It would mean more work on her part, but the tepee was too crowded already. Motioning to Nakoma and Yellow Flower to go to Snake's Lodge, she went down the path to help Standing Arrow with Little Robin. Elizabeth helped Standing Arrow carry his mother into Snake's Lodge. Little Robin was raging with fever and had obviously been sick for days. She was already covered with oozing sores. The young chief was not a coward, but Elizabeth could see the hopelessness he felt in his eyes.

"My people, they all die, we are like the leaves that fall from the trees before the snow comes. If I could find this thing, I would go and kill it," he said sadly.

Reaching out to Standing Arrow, Elizabeth laid her hand on his brow. The fever hadn't reached its peak, but she knew if Trent didn't hurry, Standing Arrow would most likely die. Her stomach knotted and she felt queasy. A tear escaped and trailed down her cheek and was followed by another.

"Be strong, my little Dove," Standing Arrow said in a gruff voice as he brushed the tears away. No words were needed. They both knew the outcome of coming to the sick lodges. Twenty-seven had died and only two had survived the illness and would carry the ugly pockmarks forever.

Elizabeth went to the stream for cool water to bathe the four newcomers before going back to the overcrowded sweaty lodge that had the smell of death. She numbly carried the lifeless bodies of the children out, but would have to wait for help to carry out the adults.

Would this ever end? Or would she watch the whole tribe slowly die? Not wanting to watch her friends suffer—but unable to leave them unattended—Elizabeth made her way back to the other lodge.

Nakoma and Standing Arrow were sleeping soundly, but Little Robin was tossing from side to side and moaning in her sleep. Yellow Flower lay awake, staring at the open center of the lodge. But she didn't see the poles that intertwined and reached out with ghostly fingers toward the heavens. Nor did she see the horsetail that told them which way the wind was blowing so they could open the smoke flaps. She didn't see the sky and clouds either. Yellow Flower was preparing in her mind to face death.

———

Ellen heard the loud distinctive crash as Daniel smashed his fist into the desktop. Quickly joining him in the study, Ellen saw him, head in hands, leaning over the desk. His broad shoulders shook slightly.

"What is it?" asked Ellen.

Shaking his head, he handed the note to Ellen.

Dear Father and Mother:

I must see Elizabeth. Trent refused to take me, so I will follow him at a distance. Elizabeth will need help caring for all the sick Indians. Please don't worry. I will be all right. We will be home as soon as we can.

Your loving daughter Katie

Ellen read the letter three times before she realized that Katie was gone and they might never see her again. Daniel held his wife for a long time while she released the pent-up tears. Both of their daughters were now somewhere out in the vast prairies and hills-out of Daniel and Ellen's reach.

Daniel considered going after Katie but soon realized he couldn't leave Ellen alone at a time like this. He was caught in the middle, not knowing which way to turn.

—◄⊷◉◈◉⊶►—

Moving on, Trent and Katie made good time but kept a wary eye for danger. The Commanche were everywhere. Small bands of warriors, painted for war, were roving the hills and valleys. The chance of two white people threading their way through the heart of Indian country seemed an impossible task. He must go slower now and make sure the enemy wasn't lurking about. The Cheyenne tribe was depending on his safe return.

He must also think of Katie, and the responsibility he felt for her safety. Stopping on a rise, Trent pointed to a valley beyond the next hill. "There, the village is in that valley, on up the draw a little ways."

"I don't see anything," replied Katie.

Chuckling, Trent said, "You won't see the village until we're almost in it."

"Let's hurry," Katie said eagerly, nudging her horse to a faster gait. They rode on for what seemed like hours to Katie but was really only a short time.

—◄⊷◉◈◉⊶►—

Elizabeth bathed Little Robin and did everything she could to make her more comfortable.

Yellow Flower seemed to have accepted her fate and was quietly waiting for the sickness to run its course. Elizabeth talked with her whenever she had a free minute. When she was busy, she was in continual prayer for the people. Her prayers always seemed to turn to Standing Arrow, Little Robin, Yellow Flower and Nakoma. Elizabeth prayed for each and every soul that lay in the sick lodges. "Pray without ceasing. That's what the Bible tells us to do," Elizabeth said out loud. It gave her strength to continue when she quoted scripture.

Little Robin lingered on in the battle of life. Elizabeth was constantly bathing her body and trying to give her relief, but the fever raged on relentlessly. Elizabeth remembered when she, soaked with sweat and burning with fever, lay in Standing Arrow's lodge. Little Robin hadn't been willing to help her or bathe her body with cool water. That made Elizabeth even more determined to make the older woman comfortable.

Going to the stream she prayed out loud. "Please Lord, send Trent back soon. I need his help and people need medicine." This prayer was on Elizabeth's mind constantly. Elizabeth walked briskly in the chilly air. It was beginning to be cool in the daytime now, and to Elizabeth it seemed even cooler after being in the sweaty lodges. She breathed deeply, enjoying the smell of the clean air.

After dipping the water, she turned and started back. Instinctively she scanned the hills for Trent, but saw nothing. *What is keeping him? He said he would be back in three days. This is only the morning of the fourth day. Don't worry yet,* she reminded herself. *What if he's hurt? Maybe*

he didn't make it. He could have been captured by roving braves"
Thoughts tortured her mind as she made the rounds and bathed fiery bodies and spoke comforting words to those that were still coherent. Elizabeth wondered if the whole tribe would die. She knew smallpox was a deadly disease.

A small moan from Yellow Flower brought Elizabeth quickly to her side. Yellow Flower was clutching her swollen abdomen. There was a look of terror in her wide dark eyes as they darted around the tepee like a caged animal looking for an escape. Yellow Flower had expected to die, taking the child safely with her to the other side. But to be separated now was more than her delirious mind could conceive. "Elizabeth," cried Yellow Flower. "My friend, bury the little one in my arms."

Elizabeth nodded numbly, knowing she couldn't lie and tell her friend that everything would be okay. The hours ticked by slowly as Yellow Flower silently labored to bring the premature baby into the world.

Elizabeth's heart ached, and her throat constricted so tightly that she could hardly swallow. She wrapped the lifeless baby boy in a small deerskin and lay it beside Yellow Flower. The exhausted mother lay on her side looking into the face of her son. She cried silently, letting the tears drop among the folds of the soft deerskin. When she could cry no more, she slept.

Elizabeth carefully took the infant from her side, wrapped it securely and covered its head. She would do as Yellow Flower had asked. The baby would remain inside until he could be buried with Yellow Flower.

Nakoma awoke and Elizabeth briefly told him about his son. Nakoma grieved silently without shedding a tear. Elizabeth knew his heart was aching—not only for his son, but also for Yellow Flower and the life they had so happily planned to share together.

Standing Arrow said little, but watched as Elizabeth cared for the sick. He knew she was exhausted yet she unselfishly cared for his people.

Chapter Eleven

Rounding the large knoll, Katie gasped at the sight stretching out before her. At least one hundred Cheyenne lodges stood proudly in the grassy valley. A stream lazily wound itself along the edge of the camp. Thickets of trees snuggled down the hillside to meet the valley floor.

Trent, however, noticed the lack of activity in the village. No children were out playing. No women were dipping water from the stream. Men weren't sitting around in groups talking, and very few lodges had smoke drifting from their open flaps. With a sinking heart, Trent urged his mount towards the sick lodges.

Dismounting, he tied his mare and took Katie's reins. "Katie," he said sternly, "we have to be prepared for the worst. Elizabeth most likely hasn't slept for days, and I'm sure she hasn't had any help."

Katie's brow furrowed as she shot him a bewildered look.

"Well, you're not in the East anymore. I just don't want you fainting or something," Trent said almost apologetically as he turned toward the path.

Katie glowered at Trent's back as she followed him into camp. *He thinks I'm a weakling,* she brooded.

Just as they reached the sick lodges, a haggard woman emerged from one of them. Straightening, Elizabeth faced Trent. A mixture of joy and relief flooded through her. "Trent. Oh, Trent, you're here!" cried Elizabeth, throwing herself into his arms.

Katie was a few steps behind Trent and didn't see Elizabeth but heard her voice. *That can't be Elizabeth. She wouldn't let a man embrace her unless—*A sinking feeling knotted in her chest. *What a fool I've been, thinking about this rugged young mountain man.* Embarrassed, but wanting to see Elizabeth, Katie stepped around Trent.

"Elizabeth," said Trent excitedly, "I brought someone to see you."

Curious, Elizabeth quickly looked around to meet the astonished eyes of her dear little sister. Reaching for her, the words tumbled out. "Katie! Oh my. How did you get here? Where are Father and Mother? Are they well?" spouted Elizabeth before she realized the look on Katie's face was a look of total repulsion, and she was backing away.

"Katie," Elizabeth said somberly, "I'm sorry you had to see me like this." The dress made of deerskins would have been enough to turn Katie's nose up but the filth and odor of vomit that clung to Elizabeth was disgusting.

Her hair was a tangle, even her hands and face were smudged with dirt.

Katie mumbled something about saddlebags, and turned quickly to the path that led back to the horses. Elizabeth was hurt and angry but she also understood. She started off to the stream for what seemed like the hundredth time. Katie dug through her saddlebags to find a bar of soap, a comb, a mirror and a clean dress for Elizabeth.

When Trent arrived to get the medicine from his saddlebags, Katie was waiting, "Why didn't you tell me?" she said hotly.

"I tried to tell you Elizabeth would be different," replied Trent. "You didn't have to be so rude to her."

"No, not that," retorted Katie.

Trent's brow furrowed. "What are you talking about?"

Sighing, Katie said, "You and Elizabeth. You didn't tell me there was something between you!"

"Between us?" Trent questioned. "There's nothing between Elizabeth and me."

Katie's eyes showed the hurt and embarrassment she felt.

"She was just glad I made it back with the medicine," replied Trent. "Besides, Elizabeth's already taken," he said and winked at Katie.

"What? Already taken? Who? Not an Indian," shouted Katie.

Laughing softly, Trent assured her he was just teasing her, as he led her back toward the tepees. "Calm down, Katie. Elizabeth doesn't always look that ragged, but she's the only one caring for the sick, Aren't you glad you came to help her?" he asked sarcastically.

Katie knew she deserved that remark. "Yes," she spoke softly. "Yes, I am," she said with confidence.

Trent smiled and winked at her. Then he turned to help Elizabeth administer medicine to Standing Arrow, Yellow Flower, Nakoma and Little Robin. Elizabeth also rubbed salve over the sores while praying it wasn't too late for the medicine to help them. Katie, still a little unsure, stood quietly at the edge of the lodge and watched Elizabeth tenderly care for these "savages," as her father called them.

Finishing up, Elizabeth led the way to the other lodge. The smell of death clung heavy inside the lodge. Trent carried the bodies of the dead out. With each trip out, he gasped for fresh air. He didn't know how Elizabeth could stay in there and care for the dying people with the smell of death so pungent. One more had died since Elizabeth's last visit, and one more child seemed to be getting better.

After everyone had been given medicine, Trent, Elizabeth and Katie began to move the sick to a clean lodge. Trent would burn the infected tepee in the morning and bury the dead.

Katie's heart went out to the children immediately. Their big soft brown eyes, round faces and raven hair didn't fit in her imagination of savages. She sang softly to them as she bathed and resettled them in clean beds.

Trent went from lodge to lodge throughout the village, taking count of the sick. To his surprise, most of the people were so scared they weren't venturing out except for water or food. The sick toll was not as high as they had expected.

By early evening they had given medicine to all the sick, and Trent instructed Elizabeth to go get some rest. He assured her Katie and he could manage for awhile.

Tired as she was, Elizabeth knew she would rest better if she were clean. She took the items Katie had brought and headed to the stream. She bathed and washed her dress in record time. As she walked down the path, Elizabeth pulled the comb through her long blonde hair repeatedly. It felt good.

She entered the chief's lodge and went directly to her buffalo robe. It seemed like an eternity since she'd slept. If she had not been so tired, she would have realized the difficulty in gathering the full cotton skirt around as she slide under the robe.

Trent and Katie worked side by side for hours, bathing, praying and comforting each person. Katie was startled when Standing Arrow spoke to her in English. "You are sister of White Dove?"

"White Dove?" questioned Katie.

"You look much like her!" replied Standing Arrow as he watched her work.

"Is that what Elizabeth is called here—White Dove?" questioned Katie.

"That is what I call her. She returned from death like a dove returns home and her skin is white," explained Standing Arrow.

"What do you mean, returned from death?"

"White Dove was wounded. She is strong and won the battle over death," replied Standing Arrow.

Katie would have liked to talk to Standing Arrow more, but needed to go to the other lodge and check on the people there before it got too dark. She decided to spend the night in the lodge where the sick children were. It would mean more work for her, but she didn't mind. She took turns holding and rocking the children—even the older ones. They seemed grateful for the attention, and Katie even got a few smiles from their tired lips.

Trent diligently tended to his patients, and by morning Little Robin's fever began to subside.

Elizabeth woke with a start. Looking around, it took a minute for her to realize where she was. She had slept well and felt refreshed. Getting to her feet, she straightened her skirts and instinctively ran her hands down to smooth the wrinkles. Making quick work of her personal hygiene, she made her way to the sick lodges.

Entering the first lodge, Elizabeth scanned the sleeping bodies and then checked each one's fever. The medicine was helping. Their temperatures didn't seem as high as before, and only one elderly woman had died during the night.

Elizabeth made her way to the other side and checked each child. Katie lay among them, a child in each arm. Bending over them carefully, Elizabeth kissed her sister softly on the cheek. The children seemed fine.

Elizabeth went to the other lodge with a dread that Yellow Flower or Little Robin would be dead. Trent looked up as Elizabeth came through the door. Relief showed on his worried face. "It's Yellow Flower. She's sobbing. I'm not much of a comfort to her."

Crossing the space between them quickly, Elizabeth knelt by Yellow Flower. She felt Yellow Flower's forehead and smoothed her tangled hair. "Yellow Flower, your fever is almost gone," cried Elizabeth happily.

Yellow Flower responded with more sobs. "What is it? What's wrong? Where is the pain?" asked Elizabeth nervously in the Cheyenne tongue.

With an anguished look in her eyes, Yellow Flower replied, "I am not going to the other side. My little son will have to go alone."

Elizabeth was so relieved that Yellow Flower was going to make it, but sad at the same time that she had lost the child. She didn't know what to say. Should she feel for the child and his travels alone to the other side or should she rejoice with the living? *This is my chance. Lord, I need your help to make her understand. Please direct my lips.*

"Yellow Flower, do you want to see your son again someday?" asked Elizabeth.

"Yes," sobbed Yellow Flower.

"Do you remember when I told you about God and his son, Jesus?"

"Yes," nodded Yellow Flower.

"Well, your son is with God. He didn't have to travel far. God took him to live in heaven with him, and if you accept Jesus as your savior, you can go to heaven when you die!"

"But I am not going to die. The fever has left me," said Yellow Flower shakily.

"Yes, but some day when you are old you will die," said Elizabeth.

"And my son . . . he will still be there with God?" asked Yellow Flower puzzled.

"Yes, he will stay there forever," replied Elizabeth. "Do you remember what I told you? You have to believe in your heart that Jesus died for your sins, and you must pray and repent of your sins, asking God to come and live in your heart, and then you will be saved! That is how you know for sure that you will go to heaven when you die," explained Elizabeth.

Yellow Flower closed her eyes tightly and folded her hands like she had seen Elizabeth do. Stumbling over the words and the unfamiliar procedure, Yellow Flower prayed calling on God to save her. When she finished, her eyes opened with peace. "I have much to learn friend," she whispered.

Elizabeth leaned over and hugged her close. Little Robin had watched and listened to the conversation. As Elizabeth knelt beside her, Little Robin asked, "Will your God take anybody to this heaven?"

Startled by Little Robin's interest, Elizabeth answered tenderly. "Yes, if you confess your sins and ask him to come in your heart, he will!"

"I want to ask him in," replied Little Robin sharply.

Elizabeth's heart was floating. Two souls had been saved. *Thank you, Lord, for using me to show these special people about you! Help me be able to teach them more about your word and to win more souls to you.*

Elizabeth was talking to Standing Arrow as she sponged his body with cool water when Katie entered.

"How is he?" asked Katie.

"Doing better. There's not much fever left."

The sisters hugged a long time and Katie told Elizabeth that she looked and smelled much better this morning. They sat and talked, unaware that Standing Arrow was watching. It amused him to hear them talk for more than an hour about what had happened since they had last seen each other.

Elizabeth glanced at Standing Arrow and saw a glimmer of humor in his dark eyes when she told Katie that Standing Arrow had threatened to give her to Snake for a wife. Elizabeth laughed and shot a smile at Standing Arrow.

Katie's reaction was quite different. "That would have been horrible," cried Katie. Standing Arrow smiled slightly and Elizabeth laughed openly.

When Katie left to check on the children, Standing Arrow spoke, "I like the dress of deerskins better."

Laughing, Elizabeth said, "It was dirty. I washed it and it's not dry yet. Katie brought me this one."

The days went by quickly now. Most of the Cheyenne tribe had survived the deadly epidemic, and life was returning to normal. Katie stayed with Elizabeth in Standing Arrow's lodge, and Little Robin waited on both of them every chance she got. Little Robin was trying to make up for treating Elizabeth so badly in the beginning.

Katie played with the children and taught them English words whenever she had free time. Most of her time was spent helping Elizabeth and the other women.

The tribe was low on food supplies and clothing for the winter because of the epidemic. The men spent time in the forest hunting and the women tanned the hides, dried meat, and gathered roots and berries. Katie didn't mind going to the forest for berries and roots, but she tried to avoid the hide tanning procedures.

"Why do you wear that dress all the time?" asked Katie with a disgusted tone in her voice.

Unsure how to answer her, Elizabeth mumbled something about how it stood up to the work better than her cotton dress. She didn't think Katie would understand that it was a lot more comfortable and not as cumbersome to move around in. She was certain Katie wouldn't understand that the leather dress pleased Standing Arrow.

The days were getting colder, and Elizabeth knew that any day now Trent would say it was time to go to Julesburg. It had been a month since he had made that long ride to bring medicine to the Cheyenne people. She knew they must go soon, or it would snow and then they would have to stay until spring. Elizabeth was anxious to see her parents, but felt uneasy about leaving the village.

She caught herself praying it would snow. *That was silly,* she thought. *I want to go back to Julesburg, don't I?*

Elizabeth spent a lot of time sitting in her favorite spot by the stream. At night Standing Arrow would come and sit with her. They spoke little but had heavy hearts, knowing time was drawing near for her departure.

"Katie will be a good wife for Trent," stated Standing Arrow.

Startled, Elizabeth turned to look at Standing Arrow, trying to read his thoughts. His face was somber and his eyes showed no amusement. Continuing, Standing Arrow said, "White Dove would make Standing Arrow a good wife."

Elizabeth's heart was breaking as she looked into the pleading dark eyes of the handsome chief. "It wouldn't work, I must go back to my people," she replied softly.

"You have earned a place with the Cheyenne. They could be your people," he countered.

Tears rimmed Elizabeth's eyes and threatened to spill over. Turning quickly to hide her tears from Standing Arrow, Elizabeth raced to the lodge. She stopped in her tracks a few steps from the door. The scream of an injured eagle pierced the night air. It left her feeling cold and shaken. Elizabeth tossed most of the night and got little rest. Each time she woke, she knew Standing Arrow was still not in the lodge.

In the following days, Elizabeth spent much of her time with Yellow Flower. Katie had brought a Bible, and Elizabeth read scriptures to Yellow Flower. It was hard for Yellow Flower to understand, and Elizabeth spent a lot of time explaining to her what the passages meant.

One chilly afternoon, Standing Arrow and Nakoma were sitting in the lodge keeping warm by the fire while Elizabeth was reading. It wasn't long before Elizabeth noticed Standing Arrow was intent on listening to her read. She decided to read through some scriptures and turned to several passages in Romans.

"As it is written, There is none righteous, no, not one" (Romans 3:10).

"For all have sinned, and come short of the glory of God" (Romans 3:23).

Skipping through Romans, Elizabeth continued.

"But God commendeth his love towards us, in that, while we were yet sinners, Christ died for us" (Romans 5:8).

"Wherefore, as by one man sin entered into the world, and death by sin; and so death passed upon all men, for that all have sinned" (Romans 5:12).

"For the wages of sin is death; but the gift of God is eternal life through Jesus Christ our Lord" (Romans 6:23).

"That if thou shalt confess with thy mouth the Lord Jesus, and shalt believe in thine heart that God hath raised him from the dead, thou shalt be saved" (Romans 10:9).

"For whosoever shall call upon the name of the Lord shall be saved" (Romans 10:13).

Puzzled, Standing Arrow asked, "This God will save anyone that asks?"

"Yes," replied Elizabeth. "All you have to do is believe that God's Son, Jesus, died and shed his blood for your sins because he was the perfect sacrifice. Confess with your mouth that Jesus Christ is Lord and ask Jesus to come into your heart."

Crossing his arms stubbornly, Standing Arrow retorted, "We have the Great Spirit. He guides us!"

Elizabeth, heavy-hearted, answered with pleading in her voice, "You think of the Great Spirit as creator, but my God, Jesus Christ is creator and savior. It is he that you have to ask him into your heart!"

Tauntingly, the hostile young chief questioned, "Our Great Spirit is not the white man's God?" His dark eyes pierced Elizabeth's gentle blue eyes like a lance aiming to kill.

Elizabeth held her ground. Lifting her chin, she was ready to meet the challenge. "Yes. There is one God over all people. In every nation, He's Jesus Christ the creator and savior for all who will receive him."

Standing Arrow continued to stare at her but didn't speak.

"Standing Arrow," Elizabeth continued, "this book is God's word and it tells us about God and what he wants us to do. God instructs us to go to other places and tell others about him. I have told you and now it's your responsibility to make sure your people know. It doesn't matter if you call him the Great Spirit or God. They are the same. You need to accept him."

The proud chief rose angrily and strode out across the camp. Elizabeth's heart ached for him. Would he ever understand?

Nakoma had sat quietly through the discussion between Standing Arrow and Elizabeth. Speaking slowly and choosing words carefully, Nakoma spoke. "This God you speak of has made Yellow Flower's heart happy and peaceful. Even after the loss of our son. My heart longs for this also!"

Elizabeth's heart leaped for joy. *Thank you, Lord. I feel honored to be used for your service.* After a few more questions, Nakoma asked Jesus to be his savior.

Elizabeth left the lodge of her dear friends with a light heart. *It will be worth it all,* she thought. Elizabeth rejoiced that they both had accepted Christ, but she also prayed that Standing Arrow would soon understand.

As he entered the lodge, Elizabeth knew immediately that Standing Arrow was still outside. She wondered if she should go and find him or if she should go to bed. Deciding that Standing Arrow needed time to think, Elizabeth crawled under the heavy buffalo robe beside Katie and prayed for Standing Arrow.

The village awoke in the early dawn to find a light blanket of frost covering the camp. Elizabeth quickly added fuel to the embers that still glowed in the fire pit. The flames leaped swiftly to consume the sticks and to bring warmth to the large tepee. To Elizabeth's surprise, Standing Arrow was still asleep. She realized he must have stayed out late.

When breakfast was about completed, Trent emerged and sat by the fire to warm himself.

"You are welcome to sleep in the lodge," said Standing Arrow.

"Thank you, but we should be leaving soon."

With a solemn face, Standing Arrow nodded. Elizabeth knew the time was coming, but she had hoped Standing Arrow would make peace with God first.

Standing Arrow and Trent spent most of the morning deciding when it would be best to leave. Trent would take the pelts he had left behind on the first trip and sell them in Julesburg. It was too late in the season for Trent to return to his camp higher up in the mountains. He would stay the winter in Julesburg. Early in the spring he would return with the items the tribe needed.

Katie was excited with the news of departure. She bustled around packing her few belongings and preparing a satchel of food for the trip. She had gained a new perspective of the people she had called "savages." They were kind and caring, and they were very protective among their people. Their lifestyle was not bad—just different from the whites. Actually, she thought the Cheyenne village got along better than any town she'd been in. Puzzled, Katie tried to think this through. But, unable to give her thoughts an answer, she shook it off and went on about her work.

Good-byes were harder this time for Elizabeth than they had been the first time. Since caring for the sick, she had made a lot of new friends. Yellow Flower clung to Elizabeth tightly and cried unashamedly. The two women had shared sorrow and joy, just like sisters.

"My friend," stammered Yellow Flower between sobs, "you hold our chief's heart captive!"

Elizabeth knew this was true, but to hear someone else say it surprised her. Looking to Yellow Flower with large pleading blue eyes, Elizabeth sought understanding. But what she saw in return was confusion and hurt. "Yellow Flower," she begged, "I must go back to my people. My father and mother are worried about Katie and me. Anyway," she continued, "it wouldn't work—we are too different."

"You have lived here almost four seasons. You are doing fine," retorted Yellow Flower.

"Yes, but if you were away from your family, you would want to return," replied Elizabeth.

Defeated, Yellow Flower told Elizabeth she would miss her and wished her happiness.

The morning of departure had come. In the two days of preparation, Elizabeth hadn't tried to speak to Standing Arrow. It was too hard. Not until they were standing in front of the lodge saying the last good-byes did Elizabeth look at Standing Arrow. Walking toward him she said softly, "I know you're not good at saying goodbye." Reaching for him, she hugged him.

To her surprise, Standing Arrow responded and hugged her in return. Quickly turning away, she mounted her horse and the little group rode out of camp. Elizabeth couldn't keep the tears from flowing. When a familiar cry of an eagle pierced the crisp morning air, she turned her mare and looked back, hoping to see Standing Arrow one last time. He was nowhere to be seen.

Mounting his horse, Standing Arrow rode swiftly to the ridge where he could watch his friends for awhile and not have them see him. As he said his last good-bye to Elizabeth, his heart swelled with pride. She turned and looked straight at him. He knew she couldn't see him, but that she was simply looking in the direction of his voice. She didn't look back long and then turned and trotted her horse to catch the others.

Standing Arrow raced back to camp and gathered a small band of eager young warriors to follow the small party, and give them protection if they needed it. He led the braves at a fast pace until they got closer and then slowed the pace. Standing Arrow caught sight of them about noon.

He noticed Trent was traveling slow and keeping a watchful eye. *My white brother is like the Cheyenne in the woods,* thought Standing Arrow proudly.

A few hours passed and Standing Arrow called the band to a halt. It was obvious that Trent knew they were being followed. The chief didn't want to worry him, so he decided to back off and follow farther behind them.

At dusk Standing Arrow went on ahead and watched as Trent carefully picked a campsite that was in a little hollow backed into the mountainside. It was closed in and gave them protection on three sides. A little spring wound its way through the edge of the open end. It was a good spot if they were attacked. They could hole up and wait for many days if need be. The only way in was to cross the stream in the open.

Standing Arrow was pleased with Trent's choice, but realized it would be harder to sneak in and talk to Trent. Going back to the braves, Standing Arrow told them their white brother had stopped for the night. Not wanting to draw attention to themselves, the warriors prepared a cold camp.

Standing Arrow slipped out and made his way back to Trent's camp. Inching slowly closer, Standing Arrow watched for movement in the camp, but all was still. The agile chief crossed the stream and slithered through the brush until he was almost upon them. He could only make out two forms in the darkness. *Where is Trent?* he wondered.

Studying the sleeping forms first, Standing Arrow crossed swiftly to Elizabeth's side. Softly he covered her mouth with one hand and laid his other arm across her arms. Elizabeth awoke with a start but kept very quiet and still. Standing Arrow could tell she was frightened, but she quickly relaxed.

He released her and Elizabeth sat up smiling. "Standing Arrow, what are you doing here?" she whispered.

"I came to talk with Trent, but he is not here."

"Not here?" questioned Elizabeth as she looked around. "He was here when we went to sleep. Maybe he is watching from the rise."

"No, my white brother is too good to let me slip into camp unnoticed," stated Standing Arrow. "He must be back-tracking to see who is following him. I will stay until he returns. You sleep."

Feeling safe with Standing Arrow there, Elizabeth drifted back to sleep immediately.

Removing his brightly ornate quill medallion, Standing Arrow slipped the leather thong over Elizabeth's head, and lay the medallion on her chest. "My spirit will go with you White Dove," he whispered.

Chapter Twelve

Listening intently, Standing Arrow was ready for battle when he heard Trent making his way back to camp. He would stay in the shadows until he knew it was Trent.

Trent was taking no chances. He eased into camp almost soundlessly. If Standing Arrow hadn't been expecting him, he might not have heard the slight disturbances of a silent night.

When Trent was close enough to hear him, Standing Arrow said quietly, "My white brother is silent in the forest."

The voice that answered was closer than Standing Arrow had thought. "My Cheyenne brother teaches well." Rising the two men moved farther back into the shadows.

"I went to your camp!" said Trent. "No one saw me, I laid in the shadows watching until I could make out seven Cheyenne braves. Why do you follow?"

"The Cheyenne people owe their lives to you and White Dove. We will follow until you reach safety," explained Standing Arrow.

—◦◦◦—

Daniel returned from work to find Ellen sobbing on the bed. As the days turned into weeks and the weeks into a month, he was having a hard time comforting her. He knew the chance of either of their daughters returning was slim. Each day that passed drove the fear and doubt deeper into their hearts.

Daniel decided that if their daughters didn't return soon, he would have to believe they were dead and try to make Ellen understand. If they were alive, reasoned Daniel, they would have been back by now. Scanning the hills for riders had became a ritual for both Ellen and Daniel. But, like always, the mountains and trees stared back, not yielding to movement of humans or animals.

When Daniel had calmed his wife somewhat, she told him that Mrs. Harrison had stopped her on the street and proceeded to tell her that it would be better to be praying that her older daughter was dead. She sure wouldn't be any good to anyone after spending that much time with those savage beasts. Furthermore, no man in his right mind would consider marrying her, and probably Katie too. Ellen began to sob again as she related the conversation to her husband.

"Please, Ellen, don't let Mrs. Harrison get you upset. You know she's a busybody and likes to cause trouble. When Trent was here, he said Elizabeth was fine," he reminded her.

"Yes, I know," sobbed Ellen. "I just want them to both come home." Sniffing, Ellen tried to control her tears.

———

The smell of coffee brought Katie and Elizabeth to their feet. Elizabeth looked around for Standing Arrow, but only Trent was by the fire. The brightly colored medallion that Standing Arrow had hung around her neck caught her eye and she gasped. How could he leave this? she wondered. She knew it was his spirit medallion.

It looked so large against her small frame. She had always thought it to be small when she saw it hanging against Standing Arrow's massive bronze chest. Still unable to believe he had left it with her, she silently fingered the tight rows of porcupine quills. It was so beautiful. She would cherish it always.

With sudden realization, Elizabeth drew in a sharp breath. His spirit medallion. He was telling her his spirit would be with her. Hugging it to her chest, she vowed to wear it always.

Breakfast was meager, and they were soon on their way. If they kept a steady pace, they would make it to Julesburg before the sun set. They saw a small band of Commanche, painted for war, and waited silently until the warriors were past and at a safe distance.

The rest of the trip was uneventful and the trio made good time. Katie told Elizabeth about town and their new house. She rambled on about people, church and stores. What Elizabeth enjoyed the most was when Katie told her how she and Trent had met. She laughed with them and then scowled at her younger sister for following Trent and almost getting herself killed.

"Amen to that," said Trent. "It scared me out of ten years of growth."

Katie sobered suddenly and apologized quickly before her eyes twinkled and she giggled.

They rode into town during the supper hour so no one was on the street. The Mayfield house was in town, but close to the edge of it. They had dismounted in front of the house and were tying their horses before anyone noticed them.

Of course, the whole town knew both of the Mayfields' daughters were with the Indians, so when Elizabeth and Trent rode in wearing deerskin clothing, moccasins and ornate paraphernalia, it caused quite a stir.

The girls and Trent managed to get to the front door before a mob could gather. Ellen, hearing the noise, rushed to the door. She stood frozen, mouth agape, as she looked at the trio coming in the door. Both girls ran to their mother and hugged her before they realized the shock on her face.

"Mama," said Elizabeth, "we're home. Mama, what's wrong?"

Just then Daniel rounded the corner. Running to their father, the sisters were enveloped by Daniel's strong arms. Hugging his daughters he laughed with joy.

"Oh, Elizabeth, we thought you were dead!" As he squeezed her even tighter, his heart swelled with happiness.

Looking at Katie, he pulled her closer and scolded sternly. "Young lady, don't you ever do anything like that again. We thought we lost both of you."

After he released the girls, they turned back to their mother. Ellen still stood in a state of shock. Elizabeth went to her, reaching for her, when her mother spoke. "Are you a wife to an Indian?"

"What?" cried Elizabeth, astounded.

"Were you forced to be a wife to one of them savages?" spat Ellen hatefully.

"Does it matter?" retorted Elizabeth. "I'm home now."

"Mrs. Harrison was right," replied Ellen repulsively. "No white man will want you now."

Angry and hurt, Elizabeth ran to the other room sobbing. Daniel, hurt and ashamed of his wife's actions stood motionless, unable to decide what to say when Trent stepped in front of Ellen.

"Mrs. Mayfield," spoke Trent evenly, "Elizabeth was not a wife to a savage. She was a guest in the chief's lodge. And she was treated like a guest." Disgusted with her misconceptions, he continued. "Elizabeth has done nothing or was forced to do anything to be ashamed of."

"Why does she have on an Indian dress?" spat Ellen.

"Mama," pleaded Katie. "The life and work of the Indians is hard. Elizabeth's dress was in rags. She made a new one with what she had."

"Ellen, you're being unreasonable. Elizabeth is alive and she's home" comforted Daniel.

Breaking down, Ellen went to her room and cried.

Katie found Elizabeth in the parlor staring out the window. With tears coursing down her cheeks, she said solemnly, "I should have stayed with the Cheyenne."

Katie hugged her. "Nonsense, Mama will be okay. She's been like this since we found out the Indians had taken you. She just needs time to adjust. Come on, let me show you the house," Katie said eagerly, dragging her sister to the bedroom. "We brought your trunks. The stage line sent them back to us."

Opening the trunk, Elizabeth picked out her favorite work dress and donned it. She tucked the medallion hanging around her neck safely inside the dress. Folding the deerskin dress carefully, she laid it in the trunk. Gathering her long silky hair, she pinned it into a bun. Stepping in front of the mirror, Elizabeth saw unhappy eyes that felt trapped in this image.

——⟨⟨⟨⟩⟩⟩——

Standing Arrow watched from a distance as the trio rode into town. He watched until he saw them draw up in front of a large white house. Unable to turn away, he waited until they had entered the house.

With a heavy heart, he turned his mount and galloped away at a space-eating stride. The warriors traveled fast the rest of that day and most of the night, stopping only briefly to let their horses rest and get a drink. When they reached the village, Standing Arrow went to his lodge and slept.

——⊸◗▥▥ᒉᒉᔿᕁᕁᕁ◖⊶——

The attack was sudden and meant to be deadly. The Commanche were tired of wandering the hills for small parties to capture. Fifty some odd braves descended on the Cheyenne camp just at the break of dawn.

With the first sounds of charging horses and whooping braves, Cheyenne dog soldiers poured from their lodges. Commanche horses thundered through the camp, bringing death wherever the riders released their arrows.

The unexpected attack had caused much confusion since there had been no time to plan. The Cheyenne women and children joined in the fight. Before the Commanche could regroup for a second run, the Cheyenne had them surrounded. Children threw rocks, women threw hatchets and men were in hand-to-hand combat.

A wild-eyed brave jumped from his horse and landed on Standing Arrow. The two men rolled over and over fighting ferociously, each trying to get control of the other. Gaining some leverage, Standing Arrow pushed the warrior backwards and pounced on him. With knife drawn, he plunged it deep into the heart of the enemy.

Removing his knife, Standing Arrow stood up, right in the path of an enemy arrow. Momentarily confused, he stiffened as his muscles paralyzed. Then came the realization that he had an arrow in his back. Before he could think the next thought, he felt himself falling. He lay conscience on the ground for a few minutes; then all went black.

When Standing Arrow awoke, he was in Nakoma's lodge. Yellow Flower was tenderly applying a poultice to the wound. His head throbbed with each beat of the drum. The death chant was being wailed throughout the camp. They had lost many warriors, women, and a few children.

"Is the wound bad?" questioned Standing Arrow.

"It is deep," replied Yellow Flower. "But I think with rest it will heal."

"Why am I in your lodge?" ask Standing Arrow. "Where is my mother?"

Yellow Flower didn't answer but looked to Nakoma. "Little Robin was killed in the battle. She was brave!" replied Nakoma.

Standing Arrow asked no more questions. His heart was full of grief for his mother, and his pain was excruciating. The next few days, Standing Arrow went in and out of consciousness. He shivered with the chills, and then burned with fever.

When he could think clearly again, his thoughts went to what Elizabeth had said about God. "Standing Arrow, you must accept him," he could hear her saying to him. He longed for her to be here with him, but was glad she hadn't been there during the attack.

Deciding to set the turmoil in his mind to rest, Standing Arrow gave his heart to God. He slept fairly comfortably for most of two days before he felt enough better to be restless.

The healing time was slow, and he had nothing to do but think. Standing Arrow began to be depressed and needed to get out of the lodge—even if it was for a just a short time. Getting to his feet, he fought off a wave of nausea and blackness. Stubbornly he walked around camp for a short time and then returned to the lodge of Nakoma and Yellow Flower, and slept soundly.

⟞⟋⟍⟋⟍⟋⟝

Katie coaxed Elizabeth to the kitchen and the sisters prepared supper together. Smelling the biscuits baking, Elizabeth realized how hungry she was for bread.

The Cheyenne people didn't eat bread. Their diet consisted of fresh meat, berries, roots and herbs. They also ate a lot of pemmican, which consisted of dried meat, berries and usually bear fat. The dried meat and the berries were ground to a powder and the bear tallow was added to form cakes. Despite the tension in the house, Elizabeth knew she would enjoy supper.

Trent and Daniel were content to sit and visit while the meal was prepared. Daniel liked the younger man, and wanted to hear all about his time spent with the Indians and how he trapped. They continued their conversation over the supper table. Elizabeth and Katie were included.

"I still can't believe Jed and I were so close. I heard your voice!" Daniel said as he shook his head, looking across the table at his sun-browned daughter. "How did you learn the language so quickly?"

Smiling shyly, she replied, "Well, when that's all you hear, you either learn it or you don't communicate. I could understand it sooner than I could speak it."

"At least you had Trent to talk to!" interjected Katie.

With a chuckle Elizabeth said, "He didn't come to the Cheyenne village until late in the summer, Standing Arrow was the only one who spoke any English."

"He risked his life to rescue you from that Commanche camp!" Daniel said as his eyes met Elizabeth's.

Lowering her gaze to the food on her plate, Elizabeth's expression changed and she answered softly, "Yes, yes he did."

Deciding it was a good time to change the subject, Trent spoke up. "Is there a boardinghouse around here?" directing the question toward Daniel. "I think I'll hole up here for the winter."

"Yes, there is," replied Daniel. "I'm glad you'll be staying. I'll take you over there after supper."

Daniel saw the smile cross his younger daughter's face as Trent and he spoke, but he missed the look that passed between Katie and Trent.

An uneasy feeling settled in Daniel's chest as he looked from one daughter to the other. Katie's reaction to Trent's staying wasn't nearly as disturbing as Elizabeth's look of despair when Standing Arrow was mentioned.

The next morning Ellen clung to Elizabeth, crying and apologizing for her behavior the night before. "I'm so thankful you're home. I've missed you. We had given up hope that we would ever see you again. Did those savages hurt you?" rambled Ellen as she sobbed.

"Only the ones that captured me!" replied Elizabeth, pulling her sleeve up to her shoulder to reveal a nasty scar that ran along the back of her arm. She assured her mother that the Cheyenne were not all savages and most had treated her kindly.

Gasping at the sight of the scar, Ellen began a new torrent of tears.

As soon as Elizabeth calmed her mother, she escaped to her room and shut the door. Opening her trunk she fingered the soft folds of her leather dress. A tear escaped and then another. Pulling the dress from the trunk Elizabeth held it close to her, breathing the smell of smoke that preserved the dress. Walking to the window that faced north, Elizabeth stared out toward the Cheyenne village. Even though the village was miles away, it seemed to calm her.

A sudden feeling of dread clutched at her heart, squeezing it painfully. With trembling fingers, Elizabeth pulled the quill medallion up and out of her dress front. She fingered the intricate circle gently. Choked with fear she ran from the house. Elizabeth covered the two blocks to the boardinghouse in record time.

The only warning Trent got was the sound of feet running down the hall, and then Elizabeth burst into his room. "Trent! Trent, something's wrong at the Cheyenne village!" cried Elizabeth.

"What?" asked Trent sharply as he rose to his feet.

"The village-something's wrong," sobbed Elizabeth.

Taking her by the shoulders, Trent shook Elizabeth gently and said firmly. "Calm down! Now tell me what is wrong?"

"I don't know . . . I just had a feeling and the medallion—it seems to make the feeling stronger. I know it sounds silly . . . I feel close to them . . . It comforts me. Something's dreadfully wrong—I just know it is," wailed Elizabeth as she babbled on about the spirit medallion. "I know it's superstitious . . . I don't really believe it has power. I just . . . It's just . . . well . . . a feeling," rambled Elizabeth as she dried her face on the sleeve of her cotton work dress. "I'm sorry to have come bursting in here like this. Please forgive me," begged Elizabeth through sniffs.

"You know you're welcome anytime," replied Trent softly. "I'm here if you need to talk."

"Thank you! I just feel like something is dreadfully wrong. I think Standing Arrow has been hurt!" cried Elizabeth.

"Standing Arrow has seven strong braves with him. He'll be all right," comforted Trent.

Still a little uneasy and unconvinced, Elizabeth slowly returned to her house.

Chapter Thirteen

Elizabeth was careful to place the medallion back inside her dress before she reached the house. She didn't want to take a chance that her mother would see it and become upset.

Two days dragged slowly by. The time seemed utterly endless to Elizabeth. Each time she thought of something to do, she was stopped short with the realization that she didn't need to scrape a hide or pound berries. She didn't even need to gather wood for the fire. Her father had a nice neat stack of firewood lined up next to the house.

She decided she could relax and work on a leather bag she had been sewing colorful quills on. But that thought too was short-lived when she realized she wouldn't need the bag. Sighing deeply, Elizabeth dug into her trunk and retrieved a tablecloth that needed to be hemmed. Sitting in the rocking chair beside the window, Elizabeth began the tedious task of small even stitches.

It wasn't long before she retired to her room and behind a closed door began to add shiny colorful quills to her deerskin bag. It gave her satisfaction to see the colors take possession of the bag. Her stitches were small and even—like on the tablecloth—but to Elizabeth it was much more rewarding to see her progress than the hidden stitches on the edge of a tablecloth.

Elizabeth couldn't shake the fears from her heart. The uncertainty was torture. She talked with Trent every chance she got, but even that didn't seem to calm her. Something must be wrong! She kept the entire village in her prayers and lifted Standing Arrow up for salvation each day.

Sunday morning, the Mayfield family buzzed around the house in preparation for church. Katie, excited to introduce Elizabeth to everyone, chattered on incessantly. Ellen and Elizabeth both seemed reserved—each with her own reasons. Daniel, however, was unaware of any out-of-the-ordinary behavior.

Elizabeth chose her pale blue dress with tiny pearl buttons that went all the way from the high collar down the front of her bodice and met with a flouncy peplum at her tiny waist. The skirt flowed freely at Elizabeth's feet, allowing ample room to walk. This organdy dress was Elizabeth's favorite, and for that reason she chose to wear it on the first outing since coming from the Cheyenne village. She felt more confident knowing she looked her best. Elizabeth could tell by her mother's reactions that she would be facing difficulties today.

Ellen was quietly praying that no one would make a fuss over Elizabeth being with the Indians so long. She had allowed Mrs. Harrison get to her before. Ellen realized now that Mrs. Harrison was just a back-biting gossip. She wouldn't make that mistake again. She believed Elizabeth and would stand by her. When the church hour rolled around, Ellen felt that her time of praying had given her the armor she needed to face the people of Julesburg.

The Mayfields met Trent at the boardinghouse before they continued the short walk to the little white church. Most of the congregation was already inside and seated when the Mayfields entered the building. A few heads turned, whispering could be heard, and more heads turned to gawk at the small group. The whispers were becoming louder now, and people openly stared.

One heavyset lady wearing a tight green dress caught Elizabeth's eye. The woman's face was a mask of repulsion. With a sigh, Elizabeth forced herself to look away.

The preacher spoke to her and held out his hand. Thankful for the diversion, Elizabeth smiled and shook his hand. Making his way to the pulpit, the preacher greeted the congregation and had began to announce a hymn when he was interrupted by the heavyset woman.

"Reverend," she said with disgust in her voice, "are you just going to allow this woman to sit in God's house and worship with good godly Christians—after she's been violated by savages for months?" She dragged the words out accusingly.

"Mrs. Harrison," replied the preacher firmly, "*if* this young woman was imposed upon, I'm sure it was against her will, unlike the gossip you so freely impose upon others."

Mrs. Harrison stood, mouth agape and eyes wide with disbelief, as the preacher spoke. With a loud "Humph," she plopped down heavily on the pew.

Trent's anger was beginning to show and Daniel's was already apparent. Katie and Ellen sat silently in a state of shock.

"Reverend," said a nervous voice.

"Yes, Miss Mayfield."

"May I speak to the people for a few minutes?" asked Elizabeth quietly.

"Yes, you may!" replied the preacher eagerly.

Taking a deep breath, Elizabeth made her way down the aisle to the front of the small church building and stood beside the pulpit. Elizabeth was more frightened when she turned to face the congregation than when she was facing death in the Cheyenne village. This, however, was a different kind of fear.

She saw a mixture of sympathy, anger towards the Cheyenne, and disgust looking back at her. If the people didn't accept her, she would be treated badly by almost everyone. She could deal with that. But if the people didn't open their hearts to what she had to say—

She let her thoughts drop and focused on new thoughts. She meticulously, with a strained voice and choppy sentences, chose her words. "I'm sure you all know I was captured by the Cheyenne last spring. I was taken to their village." Elizabeth took a deep breath and with that gained a little more courage as she continued to speak. "The men that took me purposed to torture and kill me. However, the chief would not allow it. He let me live.

"Some of the Indians are bad—just like some white men are bad—but most are good. They have children and wives. They cherish their families—just like all of you do. I was treated like a guest . . . I made friends . . . I was under the chief's protection. No one harmed me, other than the cut on my shoulder."

With pleading in her voice, Elizabeth continued. "God allowed me to go there. I was a vessel to bring the gospel to the Cheyenne. They had a great epidemic of smallpox . . . many died . . . some accepted Christ. A few are still alive that accepted Christ.

"They are eager to learn more, but they need teachers and Bibles. The Bible commands us in Matthew 28:19 and 20 *to 'go ye therefore, and teach all nations, baptizing them in the name of the Father, and of the Son, and of the Holy Ghost: Teaching them to observe all things whatsoever I have commanded you: and, lo, I am with you always, even unto the end of the world.'*

"And John 3:16 says, *"For God so loved the world that he gave his only begotten Son, that whosoever believeth in him should not perish, but have everlasting life.'*

'Whosoever' means every human being in the world. The Indians need the gospel. The seeds I've planted need to be watered and harvested." Her sentences flowed freely as she finished with pleading in her voice.

Returning to her seat, Elizabeth waited for the people to react. Faces were still fixed on the spot where Elizabeth had been. A dumbfounded, stricken look was on each face as Pastor Haines returned to the pulpit.

"Miss Mayfield is right. We do need to send a missionary!" he said.

With these words the people seemed to be jolted out of their stupor. A few were angry, but most seemed touched by Elizabeth's testimony of life with the Cheyenne. Mrs. Harrison muttered and fretted loudly, letting everyone know what she thought of the situation.

After the service several of the people spoke to Elizabeth, giving words of encouragement or asking questions about the lifestyles of the Cheyenne. Elizabeth noticed one handsome young man who hung back, waiting to visit with her. When he finally got a chance to approach her, he simply held out his hand in greeting.

"Hello, Miss Mayfield. I'm Brad Thorton!"

"Mr. Thorton, it's nice to meet you!" replied Elizabeth, expecting a question or comment. Elizabeth was bewildered when he simply touched the brim of his hat, dipping it slightly in front, then turned and strode away. She stood there watching his receding figure, wondering why he had waited so long just to introduce himself.

Daniel and Ellen had waited with Elizabeth, but Trent and Katie made their way to the Mayfield house to check on lunch. Mr. and Mrs. Mayfield knew Katie didn't need Trent's help checking on lunch, but allowed them to walk the short distance together, knowing they would be along soon.

Trent stayed most of the day, playing chess and visiting with Daniel. Both men were expert chess players and the game dragged on endlessly as far as Katie was concerned. Before Trent left, he and Katie sat on the porch swing and talked until dusk. After promising to see her the next day, Trent disappeared into the twilight.

The days passed slowly for Elizabeth. She began to feel like a caged animal and decided to go to the mercantile to look around. On the short walk to the store, Elizabeth breathed deeply, enjoying every minute of fresh air.

The store had its normal assortment of people. The town gossips were there to make sure they didn't miss anything that transpired between the people of Julesburg. Local ranchers and their wives came to fill lengthy lists of supplies. A few she saw simply seemed to be bored with the day and came just to get out of the house for a short time.

Elizabeth, being in the latter category, walked slowly around the store. She caught herself thinking about items that the Cheyenne people would like to have, or tools that would make their work easier. Ending up in the fabric section, Elizabeth was immediately drawn to the brightly colored yellow calico. *Yellow Flower would love to have a dress made of calico,* thought Elizabeth. A tear escaped, coursing slowly down her cheek as she fingered the fabric.

"I don't think yellow is your color, Miss Mayfield!" said a masculine voice.

Startled, Elizabeth turned to see the young rancher she had met at church. He looked different today. When she had seen him in his church clothes, she assumed him to be one of the town's businessmen. Today, however, he was clad in brown trousers tucked into high boots, a calico shirt, tattered hat and a well-worn leather vest. He was taller than she remembered. Towering above her, he looked down through warm green eyes.

Feeling at ease, Elizabeth wiped the wayward tear away and smiled. "Yes, you're right-yellow is not my color. But I have a friend who would love to have some yellow calico."

"An Indian friend?"

"Yes."

Brad's gaze was not one of disgust or accusation. Instead, compassion and understanding spread across his handsome, clean-shaven face. He had blonde hair, a broad smile that made his eyes look even greener, and a nose that was a little larger than it needed to be—but not so much that it took away from his good looks.

Removing his hat, Brad twirled the brim around in his fingers briefly before he spoke. "Elizabeth, may I come calling?"

"Why, yes. I suppose it would be okay." The answer came quickly and without thought.

"How about tomorrow about 7:00 P.M. Would that be okay?"

"Yes, that would be fine," replied Elizabeth.

During the walk home she began to dread what she had done. She didn't want Brad to come calling. What had she been thinking? A vivid picture of Standing Arrow haunted her mind. She wondered if he was really okay, like Trent had said, or if something dreadful had happened. Elizabeth clutched the quill medallion, drawing strength from the knowledge that it belonged to Standing Arrow. She could see him standing proudly, the medallion boldly displayed on his muscular chest. As Elizabeth continued thinking about Standing Arrow, his dark eyes pierced her soul, leaving her visibly shaken and unaware she was approaching the house.

Meeting Elizabeth at the door as he was leaving to go back to work, Daniel saw the medallion. "What is that?" he questioned.

"Standing Arrow gave it to me when I left the village."

"It's beautiful. Why didn't you show it to us?"

"I thought mother would be upset if she saw it, so I wear it under my clothes," replied Elizabeth.

"It's really important to you, isn't it?"

"Yes."

"Well, it'll be our secret—at least for the time being."

"Thank you, Father." Elizabeth stretched upward and kissed him on the cheek.

Daniel smiled and hugged her close.

"Father, do you know Brad Thorton?" asked Elizabeth thoughtfully.

"Yes. I've talked with him a few times."

"He would like to come calling tomorrow if that's all right with you!" said Elizabeth nonchalantly.

"Yes, that's fine with me. I will look forward to seeing him," said Daniel eagerly.

Daniel smiled and thought to himself: *Yes. That would be great. Maybe Brad will get her mind off of that young Indian buck.*

Elizabeth quickly tucked the medallion inside her dress before entering the house. Her outing had not done her any good. If anything, it seemed to have depressed her even more.

She returned to her room. Safely behind her closed door, she settled down to the tedious task of sewing nice even rows of porcupine quills to the soft leather. Elizabeth decided to spend as much time as possible working on the bag. She would send it to Standing Arrow as a gift when Trent returned in the spring.

Her thoughts went to other items. She would make up a package for Yellow Flower. The yellow fabric, needles and thread would be the first items on the list. Excitement filled Elizabeth as she began thinking about what she would send.

Chapter Fourteen

Standing Arrow had overdone it with his walk through camp. He decided he needed to rest more when he awoke with a raging fever, and his body shook violently with chills.

Yellow Flower checked the wound and then tucked another buffalo robe around him. She would have to try harder to keep him in bed, or he would never recover. That thought startled her! They needed him. The whole village depended on him. He was a wise chief. If he died now, the tribe would be taken over by a hot-blooded young dog soldier. They would not have quiet peaceful days if that happened.

Sitting beside the chief, Yellow Flower thought of Elizabeth while she methodically bathed Standing Arrow's forehead, checks and neck. She continued until the fever broke and Standing Arrow slept easily.

The next morning Nakoma ordered Standing Arrow to remain in bed. "I will see the people today. You must rest," he instructed.

Knowing it was for his own good, Standing Arrow smiled inwardly, but maintained a scowl on his face as Nakoma left the lodge. He was proud of his people and knew they in turn cared for him very much. It was hard to lie in bed and wait for wounds to heal.

When the sun was high and the chill was out of the air, Standing Arrow walked to the stream. Settling into Elizabeth's favorite spot, he pulled the buffalo robe closer and gazed across the rippling water. The water had a calming effect. It lulled the thoughts that nagged at his mind. He thought of Elizabeth often, wondering if she was happy. He wished she could be there with him. It would make the lonely hours pass quickly as his body healed.

Hearing Nakoma approach, he realized he had been out too long. Slowly, rising to his feet he greeted his friend. Nakoma walked him back to the warmth of the lodge.

Each day, Standing Arrow grew stronger and was able to endure more; however, he was recovering slowly—too slowly. *It is hard to heal in the wintertime when you can't get out and exercise the soreness from the muscles,* thought Standing Arrow.

Brad Thorton had faithfully called on Elizabeth every Tuesday and Saturday night. She did enjoy his company and was growing fond of him, but the image of a handsome bronze face continued to haunt her.

The weather had been good, and Brad suggested they take a ride in his buggy. Elizabeth had reluctantly agreed.

Even though there hadn't been much snow, the ground was frozen, so the horses didn't have trouble pulling the buggy. The air was cold and crisp, and the storms had died down. The couple chatted, sharing personal values and thoughts.

Elizabeth was beginning to feel at ease with the young rancher. They seemed to have much in common. The outing was fun and they laughed happily as the horses trotted slowly along the road. Passing through a large stand of trees, Brad halted the horses on a ridge. He stood up in the buggy and pointed out across the wide valley. "That's my ranch. That valley goes on for miles. It supports hundreds of cattle," he announced proudly.

"It's beautiful!" replied Elizabeth earnestly. She couldn't see the house and barns. Brad pointed to where they were located.

The valley was large, surrounded by rolling hills and small buttes. A river tumbled along the far side. It was the best ranch land for miles, according to Brad.

A rancher that had a ready supply of water had little concern about how many head of cattle he could run. With the free-range laws, the only thing a rancher needed was plenty of water and plenty of cattle. Brad Thorton had the best water supply in that country—and he had the largest herd of cattle.

Pleased that she liked it, Brad turned the horses and headed back to town. They rode along in silence.

An angry eagle call shattered the quiet. Elizabeth's stomach lurched, and her heart thudded loudly. She frantically searched the sky for eagle, turning every which way, but she couldn't locate it.

Brad, confused by her reaction, mistook it for fear. "It's okay, Elizabeth. It's just an eagle. See, up there in the tree. We're too close to her nest and she's just warning us," comforted Brad.

Seeing the eagle calmed Elizabeth considerably, but tears pooled in her blue eyes. "Please, take me home!" she begged.

Brad started the horses off at a good clip, but slapped the reins down hard when he noticed Elizabeth was sobbing.

Elizabeth didn't even notice Katie and Trent sitting on the porch when she raced past them to the safety of her bedroom. Daniel, seeing his daughter's tear-streaked face, met Brad on the porch.

With three pair of eyes questioning him, he shrugged his shoulders and looked from one to the other. "I don't know. We heard an eagle call. She was terrified of the eagle."

"Elizabeth's not afraid of an eagle," blurted Katie.

"No, but an eagle call would upset her," mumbled Trent thoughtfully. "Did she see the eagle?"

Puzzled by Trent's question, Brad answered warily. "Yes. I showed it to her. When she saw the eagle she calmed down but then she started crying."

Trent ran a work-roughened hand through his hair and shook his head. *Should I tell them?* he wondered. He had said too much not to. But would they understand?

He began slowly. "The Indians use animal calls to communicate with each other in the wilderness. Each person chooses his own call. Certain calls mean danger."

The small group on the porch was transfixed as Trent spoke. Brad was the only one beside Trent who had been in the West for any length of time, and he had not had any dealings with the Indians. He only knew what people talked about the most—that Indians raided, killed and destroyed the white man. He had been lucky and had not suffered any losses on his ranch.

He had only heard that the Indians did everything Trent talked about. But Trent had lived and hunted with them. He knew what others only speculated about. Daniel thought he had learned a lot from Jed during the search for Elizabeth, but since her return, he had realized he knew nothing of their life and culture.

Ellen had joined the group and was listening intently as Trent continued. "The eagle call is used by one man in the Cheyenne tribe—the chief."

Angrily, Brad interrupted. "Did the chief harm Elizabeth?"

"No. No, not at all. It was the chief that allowed Elizabeth to live."

"Well, what caused her to be so upset?" asked Brad hotly.

Looking from face to face, Trent knew he must tell them. With a heavy sigh he continued. "The chief-Standing Arrow—he . . . loves Elizabeth."

The faces that looked back at Trent were expressionless. They didn't seem to understand.

Trent tried again. "Standing Arrow would like to have Elizabeth for his wife!" Still the faces remained stony. Trent wondered if they even heard him. "Can't you see?" said Trent recklessly. "Elizabeth loves Standing Arrow. She won't be happy until she goes back to him!"

This brought a gasp from Ellen.

"I'm sorry I had to tell you like this, but when Elizabeth heard the eagle call, it reminded her of Standing Arrow," apologized Trent.

Brad looked stricken as he mumbled something and turned to leave.

"Mrs. Mayfield," pleaded Trent. "Standing Arrow is a good man. He would be good to Elizabeth."

"A good man," mocked Ellen, emphasizing the word man. "He's a dirty savage!"

"No, ma'am, you're wrong," spoke Trent evenly. "Standing Arrow is better than most white men and, yes, he is a man—a good man."

"Ellen," spoke Daniel patiently, "I told you about the Cheyenne brave that cut Jed and me loose. It was Standing Arrow. He didn't have to risk more time in an enemy camp for us, but he did. He saved Elizabeth, Jed and me from death in the Commanche camp."

"No daughter of mine is going to marry a thievin' dog!" spat Ellen. "I don't care who he rescued."

Shaken by her mother's outrage, Katie pleaded, "Mama, you don't know what you're talking about. The Indians are people just like us. Sure, their skin is darker, but they are no different."

Angry and confused, Ellen retreated to her room. The rest of the day was quiet and gloomy. No one knew what to say. Feeling uncomfortable, Trent made his way back to the boardinghouse.

Chapter Fifteen

Sitting alone in his tepee, Standing Arrow sat in his rightful place, directly across from the door. He stared into the flames, deep in thought. Many thoughts whirled through his mind, leaving him feeling uncertain, angry and very alone.

The winter days were long and confining. He knew he must be strong of mind and fight this sickness that left him cold and shivering and then hot and fiery. This was a mystery to his people. Some wounds healed fast, but others—sometimes even small ones-turned red and ugly with swelling. Usually, when that happened the person eventually died.

As long as he took it easy and moved around as little as possible, he seemed to get better. But when he insisted and Nakoma let him do something or go hunting, he again was in bed fighting the terrible battle of survival.

Standing Arrow missed the presence of his mother in the lodge. If she were still alive, at least he wouldn't be so lonely. Nakoma came every day to see him and bring food that Yellow Flower or one of the other women in the tribe had prepared for him. Standing Arrow looked forward to this time each day. He and Nakoma talked of the goings on in the camp and of problems that needed the chief's wisdom of the to solve.

Standing Arrow tried not to think about Elizabeth, but the days were long and he sat brooding by the fire. He tried to pray but wasn't sure if he was doing it right. He remembered that Elizabeth folded her hands, bowed her head and spoke like God was sitting right next to her. He remembered her happy laugh when he asked if he had to speak to God in English.

He was glad God knew all the different languages because right now he was tired, sick and lonely. The Cheyenne language flowed freely for him no matter how he felt, but trying to piece the English words together would make his already aching head pound with pain.

He felt trapped. He wanted to take his bow and arrows, mount his horse and ride into the woods. Nakoma had threatened to place five strong dog soldiers to stand at his tepee door to prevent him from leaving the lodge. "The Cheyenne people need you!" Nakoma had growled. "You must be strong and endure this time of healing— no matter how long."

Standing Arrow knew Nakoma was right. He must control his mind and let his body fight this battle. He must rest all day today, for tomorrow the council would meet and a new chief would be chosen for the dog soldiers. Since the death of Black Crow, the Cheyenne people didn't have a chief to lead their battles. He must be at the council because the final decision would rest on him.

Standing Arrow was certainly a capable warrior, but it was customary to have a chief over the warriors—someone who was chosen for his fighting ability—*and* a chief over the whole tribe.

He felt sure that Swift Elk would be the one chosen. Swift Elk had proven himself a worthy warrior. He was hot-blooded-always ready to fight—but he also had the wisdom of an older warrior. He would think things through before leading the warriors into a battle blindly.

Standing Arrow thought back to Black Crow and his faithful followers. They had caused havoc on the prairie. He knew that if they had not died from the fever and sores, Black Crow and his men would have died a slow death at the hands of the Commanche. In order to keep peace with the neighboring tribes, Standing Arrow would have sacrificed the renegades to appease the Commanche. He would have had to choose a new chief of the dog soldiers anyway. Black Crow had not been worthy of the job.

The Commanche had satisfied their thirst for blood when they attacked the Cheyenne encampment. Standing Arrow was glad Elizabeth wasn't there when the village was attacked; however, he was tempted to give in to Yellow Flower's pleading and let Nakoma and some of the warriors go to the white village and bring Elizabeth back. Yellow Flower was sure Standing Arrow would recover faster if Elizabeth were there. The proud, young chief held firm, replying that it was too dangerous for Elizabeth to travel in the season of the snow.

Standing Arrow knew he would make the journey himself at the first signs of thawing. He must tell Elizabeth that he had asked her God to live in his heart—to be his God. He knew she didn't want to live with the Cheyenne and be his wife, but he wanted to see her again and ask her one more time. And this time, he would say a proper good-bye.

Chapter Sixteen

In the days that followed, Brad came over for supper a few times, and he and Elizabeth went on a few outings. Although her heart was not in it, she did enjoy Brad's company. And it pleased her mother when she spent time with Brad.

Maybe if she tried hard enough, she could forget Standing Arrow and live a normal life with someone like Brad Thorton. She would have to try harder to get to know him. *What could possibly be wrong with him?* she asked herself. He shared her faith in God. He was a pleasant enough person. He was handsome, and he had a wonderful ranch. A girl could do a lot worse in this wild country. Maybe, just maybe, she could learn to love Brad.

The day was crisp, but spring was in the air. Elizabeth happily hummed to herself as she pinned her hair up into a tight bun. She had made up her mind to have a wonderful time with Brad this afternoon. She loved to ride, and Brad had promised to take her for a long ride. Elizabeth smiled to herself as she thought how kind and gentle he was.

She knew that, even if he hadn't asked her, Brad wanted her to be his wife. For the first time Elizabeth wondered if she was crazy. How long would she hold on to the image of Standing Arrow? Maybe she should just marry Brad and live a normal life.

Reaching for the colorful medallion, Elizabeth lifted it over her head carefully and laid it on her nightstand. She would send it back to Standing Arrow with Trent when he left in the spring.

Ellen called to Elizabeth just as she was tucking the last of the wayward curls into her bun.

"Yes, mother."

"Would you please run to the store for me?"

"Yes, of course. What do you need?"

"I have a list for you," replied Ellen.

"I'll be right out."

With one last glimpse in the mirror, Elizabeth's eyes rested on the quill medallion. Without another thought, Elizabeth placed it around her neck, clutching it briefly before hiding it inside her bodice. She couldn't part with the medallion yet.

Normal life! I'm crazy for trying to make myself believe that. That's why I wanted to come west—I was tired of normal! she reminded herself. With a heavy sigh, she headed out of the house. It was a beautiful day. Signs of spring were beginning to show everywhere. Little sprigs of bright green grass were poking through the dried clumps of last year's growth. Birds chirped and fluttered around. The air was beginning to warm.

Elizabeth envisioned the Cheyenne children playing and running in the spring air after a long cold winter of sitting in the lodges by the fire. She longed to see them all again. She would love to deliver the package she was putting together to Yellow Flower herself. But she knew it would only be harder to leave again. *If only Standing Arrow would accept Christ, I would go and marry him,* she caught herself thinking.

Her thoughts startled her. Elizabeth pulled her shawl about her shoulders and walked the short distance to the general store.

Humming softly to herself, she thought of things she still needed to do. Soon she would need to get the things ready for Trent to take to Yellow Flower. *Standing Arrow will be proud to wear the bag I made for him.* Elizabeth smiled at the thought. And then a frown came to her lips. She would like to give it to him herself!

Her thoughts were cut off instantly when a loud clear eagle call echoed down from the ridge. Elizabeth froze only for an instant before she broke into a run. She wasn't dressed for climbing the ridge, but she didn't care. She just wanted to get to the top. She scrambled over rocks and climbed higher and higher. When she wasn't using her hands to help her move along more quickly, she was using her fingers to pull pins from her hair, letting it tumble down her back.

She was breathing heavily by the time she reached the rim. Quickly heading for the stand of cottonwoods, she scanned their depth, looking for a sign of where Standing Arrow might be. Elizabeth's heart pounded excitedly.

Before she could reach the trees, a buckskin-clad form on a horse emerged. Standing Arrow was dressed in his finest paraphernalia. Eagle feathers hung from his shiny black hair that fell against the golden buckskin shirt. The shirt was adorned with red, yellow, orange and green porcupine quills and had small tufts of hair sewn along the strips of quills. A few large beads hung around his neck along with a sheathed knife. His full leggings and moccasins were also colorful with their quills and long fringe decoration. A quiver full of arrows and a bow hung casually across his shoulder and down his back.

It took Elizabeth only a few seconds to drink in the magnificent sight of Standing Arrow waiting for her. As she closed the distance between them, Standing Arrow dismounted and waited. Elizabeth stopped a few feet from him, unsure of Cheyenne tradition in a situation like this. A broad smile covered Standing Arrow's handsome bronze face, and his eyes twinkled warmly.

"Your God lives in my heart and is my God," he announced.

Elizabeth was overjoyed. That was all the encouragement she needed to willingly stepped into Standing Arrow's embrace. With her head on his chest she could hear his heart beating and feel the warmth of his body.

This was the feeling she knew she would have to have to marry a man. And she knew then that she didn't feel that way about Brad Thorton. It would be wrong for her to marry Brad, pretending to love him. It wouldn't be fair to Brad either.

With complete assurance, Elizabeth stepped back and gathered her shawl, pulling it tight across her back and holding onto the edges. She wrapped her arms around Standing Arrow, covering him with the shawl.

"Does my little dove know the meaning of this?" asked Standing Arrow seriously.

Looking into his dark eyes steadily, Elizabeth answered. "Yes, I do know the meaning. If you still want me!"

Standing Arrow's face lit up as he reared back and let out a loud joyful eagle call. Pulling Elizabeth to him, he hugged her tightly. Unaware and unconcerned about danger, Standing Arrow chatted happily with Elizabeth. He had been so happy to see Elizabeth that he had let down his guard.

Brad topped the rise from the south that overlooked the town. He had always liked the first glimpse of Julesburg. The houses and stores nestled nicely in the valley. People moved about, horses stomped at the hitching rails. He could see the whole town from this here. Reining in, he paused to look across the town.

Just as he spotted Elizabeth crossing the street, a shrill eagle call split the silence, leaving an eeriness in the air. Puzzled, he watched as Elizabeth ran for the north ridge and scrambled up the side of it. His puzzlement then turned to anger.

When Brad realized what was happening, his stomach felt heavy and his muscles tightened. He could see nothing, but he knew that dirty savage was out there— and Elizabeth was going to see him. Wildly, Brad raced his mare down into the valley.

He skirted the north ridge and ascended just beyond were Elizabeth had disappeared. Slowing, he worked his mare along the edge of the trees until he found his prey.

Brad's blood turned icy and common sense left him when he saw the couple embracing. Raising his rifle, he sighted in and held it steady, waiting until Elizabeth released her hold on the Indian. *That was odd,* he thought. *It should be the other way around. Why did Elizabeth have her arms around him?*

Watching intently for Elizabeth to remove her arms, Brad heard another shrill eagle call split the air. He felt an uneasy presence. Quickly turning, his heart leaped and his face went white. Seven Cheyenne warriors had him circled, their spears aimed at his heart.

Common sense returned quickly, and by the hard looks on the braves' faces, Brad realized his only choice was to comply. He slowly lowered his rifle and placed it on the ground at his feet. Straightening slowly, he lifted both hands in the air. The warriors motioned him to walk toward Standing Arrow and Elizabeth. Reluctantly, he obeyed.

Standing Arrow turned as the small group broke through the last row of trees. His expression became grave. Elizabeth recognized Brad, and knowing the ways of the Cheyenne, realized he was in a bad way.

When they drew up in front of Standing Arrow, Elizabeth spoke. "Brad, what happened? What were you doing?"

Before he could answer, Nakoma spoke angrily to Standing Arrow, telling him they had caught the white man with a rifle cocked and aimed, waiting to get a shot at him.

Elizabeth, unable to believe what she had heard, looked at Brad. "You were going to shoot Standing Arrow?"

"How can you understand that jibberish?" retorted Brad defiantly.

Angry and hurt, Elizabeth replied. "I lived with them for most of a year. You either learn it or you don't speak to anyone." Turning to Standing Arrow, Elizabeth spoke to him in Cheyenne. "Please don't harm Brad. He's a good man."

"He was trying to kill me!" retorted Standing Arrow. The conversation went back and forth for some time, and even though Brad couldn't understand, he could see the closeness between the two.

"Can't you let Trent take care of him until you've reached safety?" pleaded Elizabeth.

Against his better judgment, and because he was exhausted, Standing Arrow gave in to Elizabeth's pleas. Turning to the warriors, Standing Arrow Spoke to Nakoma. "Tie him up, and watch him closely."

Staring for a moment in disbelief at their chief, they reluctantly obeyed. Roughly, they bound Brad and started dragging him off into the thick stand of trees.

"Elizabeth-Elizabeth!" shouted Brad, dragging out the words. "What are they going to do with me?"

The smile of victory faded from her face as she turned to face Brad. "They will not kill you if you cooperate, but you will have to stay tied up until they leave. Trent will let you go," she said almost apologetically. She was beginning to be angry and wondered if he didn't deserve to die. She quickly brushed that thought away and reminded herself of what it said in Romans 3:10: "*There is none righteous, no, not one.*"

Standing Arrow came up behind her leading Brad's mare. "Ride and find Trent. We must talk," commanded Standing Arrow.

Climbing atop the black horse, Elizabeth reined the mare in the direction of town. As the beats of the horse's hooves receded in the distance, Standing Arrow and Brad faced each other. Both had swelled chests and clenched jaws, and their eyes held a challenge.

"Elizabeth wishes you to live," spoke Standing Arrow thickly in English. "So don't give me a reason to kill you." Standing Arrow turned abruptly and strode away.

Elizabeth rode into town at a fast clip. Reining in at the boardinghouse, she dismounted and strode in to find Trent in his room. Elizabeth explained what had happened while he got ready to leave and they were soon out the door.

"I need to stop at the preacher's house. It should only take a minute or two," said Trent quickly as they headed into the street.

Nodding, Elizabeth remembered that she was supposed to go to the store for her mother. "I'll go to the general store while you're at Preacher Haines' houses."

Inside the store she quickly found the items on the list and hurried out the door without a word to anyone.

When Elizabeth reached the house and had put away the supplies, she then packed some things in a saddlebag. She found Katie in her room sewing. "Katie, come quick. Standing Arrow, Nakoma and some of the dog soldiers are on the north ridge. Trent's on his way. Do you want to ride up with us?"

Katie always enjoyed adventure and time spent with Trent, so she needed no urging. The sisters had their horses saddled and ready when Trent arrived.

"Good news!" called Trent as the girls approached.

Elizabeth's brow furrowed as she questioned him. "What is it?"

Smiling broadly, Trent began. "Preacher Haines has agreed to let a family go to the Cheyenne village and teach the people about God. He is going to send Bibles and other books to teach them how to read and write."

"That's wonderful!" cried Elizabeth. "But who will go?"

"Well, hold on now," laughed Trent. "I have to get Standing Arrow to agree to it first and then Pastor Haines will decide who goes. He has two families that are willing."

Elizabeth was speechless. She hadn't known that Preacher Haines was planning to send missionaries from their own little church to the Cheyenne village. Her heart filled with pride. "Do you know which families?" she asked.

"Yes. One is your father."

"My father?" chuckled Elizabeth. You're not serious."

"Yes, he thought it might help your mother accept Standing Arrow more easily if she spent time at the village."

"Accept him?"

Trent looked a little embarrassed. "Yes, your father knows you won't be happy with anyone else."

"He said that?"

Trent nodded.

"Well," laughed Elizabeth as she looked at Trent. "I guess we'll just have to have a double wedding at the Cheyenne village."

The sisters laughed, enjoying the teasing, but Trent's dark tan deepened.

Nakoma greeted the trio before they reached the others and rode the rest of the way with them.

"Where is Standing Arrow?" asked Elizabeth.

"Sleeping."

"Sleeping?" she repeated with concern in her voice.

"Yes, he has been very sick all winter. The Commanche attacked the village early in the morning on the day we returned from here. Standing Arrow took an arrow in his back. It was very deep. Yellow Flower has been caring for him daily, but he does not always obey her words. His body raged with fever for many days, and he has been weak like a child. Little Robin was killed in the battle . . . This trip was hard for him."

"Why didn't someone come and get me?" asked Elizabeth.

Nakoma sighed deeply. "Yellow Flower pleaded, and I even offered to ride for you myself, but Standing Arrow said it was too dangerous in the winter to travel through Commanche territories, and he would not allow us to put your life in danger."

Elizabeth's heart sank. She had known something was wrong—she had felt it. She should have gone back to the village on her own.

Dismounting, she picketed her horse and made her way to where Standing Arrow was resting. She quietly sat beside him and watched him sleep. She knew by his breathing that he was aware of her presence.

Trent talked with Brad, assuring him that if Standing Arrow said he wouldn't kill him, he wouldn't. Standing Arrow's word was good. "It was a foolish thing you did. You're a very lucky man. To kill a chief is certain death—a slow death. Don't anger them further," warned Trent.

Brad was angry and sullen. He could not believe how at ease Trent, Elizabeth and Katie were with these savages. He felt like they had betrayed him.

Elizabeth and Katie prepared a meal for the men from the supplies Elizabeth had packed. She had brought two big loaves of fresh baked bread, a crock of butter and chokecherry jelly. One of the braves had killed a deer and had the hindquarter roasting on the fire. For a special treat Elizabeth had packed a chocolate cake and two jars of peaches.

After slicing the bread, she spread generous amounts of butter on each piece and then an equal amount of jelly. Watching the warriors devour the strange new food, Elizabeth couldn't wait to let them taste the peaches and chocolate cake. Standing Arrow ate, but not with enthusiasm.

Elizabeth kept an unnoticed eye on him and decided she had better take a look at his wound. She had been too excited to see him, and had not noticed before how thin he was and that his usual bronze glow had paled.

Reluctantly he allowed Elizabeth to lift his shirt and exam the wound. The gasp escaped her lips before she could stop it. The hole was swollen and oozing and there were deep red streaks coming away from the ugly wound.

"Standing Arrow, this should be healed by now. You have a terrible infection," scolded Elizabeth. "You haven't been taking it easy. Now you need medicine!"

"It will heal," replied Standing Arrow flatly as he struggled to get his buckskin shirt back into place.

Calling Trent over, Elizabeth again lifted Standing Arrow's shirt carefully, showing him the ugly wound. The look that passed between them was the same. "He needs a doctor—and quick," they said together.

Elizabeth carefully repositioned Standing Arrow's shirt.

Trent paced around for a few minutes and then slipped off unnoticed by everyone except Elizabeth.

The warriors continued to eat until the food was gone and they were stuffed.

Nakoma was worried about Standing Arrow. He was sleeping again. He shouldn't have let him come. He didn't understand why the wound wasn't healing. What if Standing Arrow didn't recover? What if he died? He knew the burden would rest on him forever. He felt responsible for allowing Standing Arrow to come on this trip. All these thoughts went round in his mind until he thought he would go crazy.

With an empty chuckle, he realized that he couldn't have stopped him even if he had been more persistent. Standing Arrow was the chief and he did what he wanted and made his own decisions. But somehow it seemed that he should have been able to persuade him not to come.

Trent returned before dusk with the doctor. The dog soldiers immediately became tense and ready to protect their chief from the stranger that Trent had brought to camp.

Elizabeth gently woke Standing Arrow and told him that Trent had brought a doctor. Standing Arrow's English was somewhat limited, and most of the warriors didn't even understand English, so Elizabeth spoke to him in Cheyenne.

The warriors circled Standing Arrow and watched as the doctor worked on him.

The doctor felt trapped and was very nervous. His hands shook as he lifted the buckskin shirt. He couldn't see the scowl on Standing Arrow's face but was constantly aware of the circle of warriors around them. They seemed to be getting closer and closer. The closer they came, the more the doctor shook.

Elizabeth talked as the doctor worked, explaining everything he was doing. She even warned him that the disinfectant would burn. Standing Arrow sat stone-faced through the whole ordeal, never flinching or showing any emotion on his face. The doctor gave him an antibiotic and recommended that he sleep as much as he could. Elizabeth explained to Standing Arrow that he must take the medicine every day for at least ten sleeps.

When the doctor left, emotion again began to flicker in Standing Arrow's eyes. "When will you come to the village and be my wife?" he asked.

"Soon. But you need to get well first." They talked for a short time before Katie and Elizabeth headed back to town.

Trent stayed and talked with Standing Arrow about the possibility of one or two families coming to the Cheyenne village to teach the Bible to his people. At last, with the details worked out, the men found a spot to bed down for the night.

Trent lay on his blanket, staring up at the stars thinking. *I should have gone to check on Brad and given him something to eat and drink. Oh well, maybe it will do him good to go hungry one night. He should be grateful he's alive.* Trent rolled over and drifted into a sound sleep.

The warriors took turns on watch, but Standing Arrow slept soundly all night. In the morning he felt much better. *Could it be that the white man's medicine was this strong?* thought Standing Arrow as he stretched his sore muscles. Scanning the countryside around them, Standing Arrow's eyes rested on two riders silhouetted by the colorful pink and blue hues of the rising sin. He was happy to see one of the riders was Elizabeth, but he didn't recognize the other person. Waiting patiently as they approached, Standing Arrow thought the man seemed familiar, but couldn't think of where he had seen him.

Elizabeth dismounted and approached Standing Arrow. "Standing Arrow, this is my father, Daniel Mayfield," she said as she introduced them. "Father, this is Standing Arrow."

Daniel stuck out his hand and Standing Arrow grasped it firmly. Trent had told him of some of the white man's customs—the handshake had been one of them.

"Thank you for cutting us loose in the Commanche camp," Daniel said.

Nodding, Standing Arrow acknowledged the thanks. "Elizabeth is worth many strong ponies!" he said.

Puzzled and not knowing how to answer, Daniel looked to Elizabeth for help. Elizabeth, however, wasn't much help. She laughed softly and her eyes twinkled as she waited to see what her father would say.

"Uh . . . yes she *is* worth many strong ponies" replied Daniel.

Their eyes held momentarily and Standing Arrow considered the matter confirmed.

Elizabeth fixed breakfast while the men talked and made plans. After breakfast Standing Arrow said it was time for them to return to the village. Elizabeth made her way inconspicuously to Nakoma's side. Looking at him with worried eyes, she spoke softly to Nakoma. "You will take it easy on the way back, won't you?"

"I will watch him closely," Nakoma assured her in a firm voice. "I will not let harm come to him."

"He shouldn't be traveling yet. He needs a lot of sleep!" pleaded Elizabeth.

"Do not worry. He is our chief. We will take good care of him," promised Nakoma gently.

"You will make sure he takes the medicine the doctor gave him?"

"I will."

Feeling a little better, Elizabeth nodded her head in thanks and handed a small package to Nakoma. "This is for Yellow Flower. Tell her I miss her and tell her I will be coming to the village soon."

"She will be happy to have you back at the village." Nakoma nodded and stowed the package in his saddlebag.

It was very difficult for Elizabeth to let Standing Arrow go without her. Her heart screamed with every minute that passed. She didn't know if she could wait the two weeks until the pastor had an organized party ready to make the journey across the prairie to the Cheyenne encampment.

As the riders disappeared, her heart felt tight and her stomach heavy. She couldn't make her voice work through her constricted throat. Elizabeth stood unmoving until Standing Arrow could no longer be seen. It was then that she realized Trent was standing beside her with his arm around her shoulders.

As the tears began to course their way down her cheeks, she was glad Trent was there. It was good to have a close friend that understood. Trent held her while she cried herself out and then escorted her home, before returning to the ridge to release Brad.

To Elizabeth, the two weeks seemed to drag by, but the pastor and other people preparing for the journey seemed to think two weeks was enough time. Pastor Haines would not be going, but was helping with the supply list.

To Elizabeth's surprise, her mother was actually excited to go. She loved children and kept talking about teaching "those poor deprived and neglected children."

Chuckling to herself, Elizabeth knew her mother was in for a big surprise. The Cheyenne might live a different lifestyle than the whites, but to deprive or neglect their children was not their way. Children were regarded highly among the Cheyenne tribe.

Chapter Seventeen

he supplies were sorted and packed carefully into three wagons. Personal items were of the least importance and therefore each person was limited to one valise. Two of the wagons were burdened with flour, sugar, beans, dried fruit, bacon and an assortment of other foods needed. The last wagon carried Bibles, books, tools, medicine and trade items.

Elizabeth packed each item that she had carefully selected for Yellow Flower—two different bolts of yellow calico, a large pair of scissors, needles and thread, yards of colorful silk ribbon, an assortment of buttons and a large cooking pot. She then packed some things for Standing Arrow—a large cooking pot, a few knives, two tin cups and some other items she would need when she became his wife. She would save the quill bag to give him as a wedding present.

Next she stocked her sewing kit, making sure she had scissors, needles, thread and even a few pieces of calico. Last of all she took the thick colorful quilt from her bed and placed it among the items to be packed.

The day of departure had arrived. Sam and Mary Larson were seated on the wagon box. Their three children—Laban, Sarah and Ellie—were perched on boxes in the wagon bed. The children were ready and anxious for a new life with the Cheyenne. Laban was an energetic eight-year-old that was always looking for excitement. His face beamed with the adventure as the wagons creaked out of town.

Sarah at the age of six, was quite the opposite. She was quiet and serene. Ellie was only four, but seemed to be leaning more toward her brother's personality than that of her somber sister.

Mr. Larson was a rugged adventuresome man. And his wife, never complaining, followed along. Mary Larson loved children of all ages and planned to learn the Cheyenne ways quickly in order to better teach them.

The Mayfields drove the second wagon. Ellen sat happily at Daniel's side. Both of their daughters were in the wagon bed. The family Ellen had thought she had lost was together again. They were going as a family to minister to the "savages" that had caused her so much grief.

Trent rode his black mare ahead of the wagons, scouting and watching for any sign of trouble. The small group of wagons trundled slowly across the grassy prairie.

Elizabeth gazed over the countryside, her eyes lingering in the direction they were traveling. How she wished she could just mount her mare and race off at a fast clip. She could be at the village tomorrow if she did. At the pace they were going, it would most likely take five or six days. Sighing she tried to think about other things. She was worried about Standing Arrow. The trip back would have been hard on him.

—⟞⟍⟋⟍⟞—

Standing Arrow had gained most of his strength back and was feeling better than he had all winter. He wanted to go for a hunt, but didn't want to be gone when Elizabeth and the others arrived.

He had told the tribe that White Dove, her family and another family would be coming to the village to teach them about the Bible and God. However, he was saving the announcement of their marriage until Elizabeth could be with him. The children were excited knowing they would see Elizabeth and Katie again, and most of the women were busy preparing a feast for their arrival.

Enough time has passed—they should be here soon, thought Standing Arrow as he paced briskly around camp waiting for them.

Some of the older women sat around and watched as Standing Arrow restlessly moved about.

"Our chief is lonely," said one.

"Yes, he needs a wife," another said. The others agreed.

"If he is too shy to take a wife, we will choose one for him," one of them suggested.

"Yes. It is not good for the chief to be lonely," another agreed.

As the elder women of the tribe planned, they thought about all the eligible young maidens that could possibly be a wife for their chief.

Standing Arrow, unaware of their intentions, couldn't stay in camp any longer. Gathering a few restless braves and Nakoma, he headed out to meet the group of wagons.

⋙✦⋘

Trent motioned for the three wagons to pull over on a flat grassy knoll and make camp. The travelers, tired from the first day of their journey, were more than ready to call it a day. As tired as Elizabeth was, she was reluctant to stop. She would have liked to jump on her mare's back and race wildly across the hills until she reached the Cheyenne village.

The women quickly busied themselves with supper preparations, while the men tended to the animals and checked the wagons. Laban and Sarah were sent to gather wood for the cooking fires, and were instructed not to wander too far from camp.

Elizabeth managed to keep her anxiety under control and dropped off to sleep soon after the clean up from the meal was done. However, she was the first to rise and get things moving in the early dawn.

When the wagons resumed their steady rhythm of rocking, creaking and jostling, Elizabeth felt like they were once again making some progress. She didn't know if she could endure the trip at this slow monotonous pace. Riding in the wagon made every muscle and joint in her body ache. She decided it was time to ride her horse.

Riding ahead on her mare, Elizabeth stopped on a knoll to look out across the prairie and breathed in the fresh air. The wind softly blew tendrils of her hair—the ones that had escaped her tight bun—about her face. Her heart was swelled with happiness. Taking a few more minutes, she thanked God for the beautiful countryside, for her family and friends—but most of all for using her to tell the Cheyenne people about God and his love for everyone.

When the others had caught up to her, she rode close to her family's wagon. She was surprised with the words her mother spoke. "You really love that Indian, don't you?"

A smile played across Elizabeth's lips as she answered. "Yes, mother. I really love him."

"Your father said you want to marry him. Is this true?"

Again, the same smile clung to her lips. "Yes." Elizabeth knew as she replied that her mother wasn't very happy about the situation, but she thought she might be softening a little.

It was early afternoon when Trent rode up beside Elizabeth. He had ridden on ahead a bit and had just returned. A broad smile crossed his face as he spoke. "Just over that rise is a welcoming party, and Standing Arrow is leading it."

Needing no urging, Elizabeth started her mount out at a quick space-eating stride. It wasn't long before she could see the small group of warriors steadily making their way toward the wagons. At almost the same time Elizabeth saw the riders, one broke away from the group and came on at a gallop.

When the wagons crested the hill, Standing Arrow and Elizabeth were leading their ponies and slowly walking as they talked. It didn't take long for the lumbering wagons to overtake them.

Elizabeth was excited for her mother to meet Standing Arrow. She was sure that when her mother met him she would like him. Standing Arrow, one of the bravest Cheyenne warriors, was a little reluctant to meet Ellen. He knew that if she disapproved, Elizabeth would not go against her parents' wishes. Standing Arrow thought he would rather fight a grizzly bear than meet an angry mother. But he knew he must if he wanted Elizabeth for his wife.

Daniel drove the wagon steadily on as they overtook Standing Arrow and Elizabeth. Ellen stared at the back of Standing Arrow and noticed his broad shoulders and how tall and proudly he carried himself. She also noticed his long shiny black hair that fell loosely down his back, almost reaching his waist. Two feathers fluttered freely from the side of his head and the leather clothes he wore seemed to be alive as the fringe swayed and bounced with each step he took.

Daniel stopped the wagon as he pulled up beside them. Standing Arrow, smiling and remembering the white man's greeting, reached for Daniel's hand.

"We meet again," the chief said.

"Yes. It's good to see you are feeling better," replied Daniel while he shook his hand.

Standing Arrow then reached for Ellen's hand and shook it gently, saying "Mother of Elizabeth?"

Ellen nodded. "Yes," she mumbled. She was amazed. He didn't look at all like the picture she had conjured up in her mind. He was young, handsome, *clean*, and polite. He didn't look like a wild beast at all. Shame overcame her immediately, and the look of despair covered her face.

Standing Arrow, seeing her expression, mistook the meaning of it and decided he had better stay as far away as he could—at least for awhile.

Turning swiftly, Standing Arrow leaped effortlessly onto his pony's back. Looking down at Elizabeth, he gruffly said, "I tell friends." He turned his mount around and was galloping across the grassy meadows before Elizabeth could reply.

With a heavy heart, Elizabeth hung her head and walked while leading her mare. She fell in behind the last wagon and trudged on.

Daniel, taking in the whole scene, was angry. One look at Ellen was all she needed to know his anger was directed toward her. With a quick snap of his wrist he laid the reins wickedly across the mule's back. The wagon lurched violently and Daniel pulled in behind the last wagon.

The Cheyenne camp was alive with excitement. Everyone was busy with preparations for the feast they'd have when the small group arrived.

News was traveling quickly that the chief would also pick a wife. The elderly women of the tribe had chosen two eligible maidens for Standing Arrow to choose between. Excitement spread throughout the entire village.

When the news about the chief having to choose a wife reached Yellow Flower, she was angry. It was too late now for her to do anything about it. The whole village had been notified: Standing Arrow must now choose a wife if he wanted to remain the chief of the Cheyenne. To refuse would be an insult to the people. Yellow Flower couldn't see any way out.

She knew it wouldn't do any good to talk to the young maidens. For them to refuse to marry a chief was unheard of—especially one as kind and handsome as Standing Arrow. Yellow Flower's heart was heavy as she waited for the arrival of her friends. *I must think of something. Surely there is a way out of this.*

But no matter what she came up with, Yellow Flower couldn't see a way out. Her anger rose further when Yellow Flower realized Rain Song was already promised to Swift Elk, a high warrior who was riding with Standing Arrow. Rain Song was one of the maidens the older women had chosen for Standing Arrow. *That would be a bad thing,* thought Yellow Flower shaking her head.

She decided the only thing she could do was what Elizabeth had taught her-pray! *Oh Lord! Please help this problem to work itself out. You know what is best for Standing Arrow. Please help this to be your will!*

Yellow Flower kept the problem—and her simple prayer—constantly in her mind as she did her daily chores.

Chapter Eighteen

With the wagons pulled into positions and fires being started, the travelers began preparations for the evening meal.

Standing Arrow rode into their camp carrying a young doe across his pony's back. He rode boldly to the Mayfields' fire and deposited the deer at Ellen's feet.

Ellen knew she must try really hard to make friends with this proud, young chief. *What does he want me to do with it?* she wondered.

When Daniel brought home a deer, it was already skinned and quartered. This one hadn't even been skinned. It lay there with dirt caked on its open eyes and its tongue flopping out the side of its mouth. *At least the guts are removed,* thought Ellen.

As her eyes moved over the deer and then up to meet Standing Arrow's piercing dark eyes, she realized he was holding something out to her.

Standing Arrow saw the question in her eyes. With a forced smile, he said, "Gift," as he thrust his hand towards Ellen. "Gift to mother of Elizabeth. It is still warm." He extended his arm out further.

Ellen looked from his deep dark eyes to his outstretched hand. What see saw sent shivers through her body. A dark red blob of meat hung in Standing Arrow's hand. Blood that was almost black ran down his arm and dripped to the ground.

"Take it," coached Daniel softly.

Ellen, still in a daze, didn't move.

"Take it," repeated Daniel sternly.

Elizabeth broke the silence. "Mother, it's just the liver from the deer. If you eat it when its warm, it's good for you. Most warriors eat it as soon as they kill an animal. It is as honor for a warrior to bring the warm liver from his kill and present it as a gift."

Ellen turned to Elizabeth, "You eat it raw?" she said incredulously.

"Yes, Mama, we all get at least a bite."

Panic-stricken, Ellen turned her gaze back to Standing Arrow. "Thank you . . . for the . . . gift," she choked out. "As . . . our guest . . . we would . . . like for you . . . to have the first . . . bite."

Amusement and embarrassment flickered in Standing Arrow's eyes. He had made a bad choice for a gift. This was obviously not a white man's custom. But he would make the best of it. Without taking his eyes off Ellen, he bit off a large juicy chunk, smiling as he chewed and swallowed it.

Then he passed it to Trent and then Daniel, who each did likewise.

It was then Elizabeth's turn. She took a bite and then passed it to Katie. Katie took a small bite and handed it to her mother.

Ellen couldn't believe her eyes. They were all standing there with blood dripping from their lips and chins. Thinking she was going mad, she grabbed the meat and bit into it like a ravished dog and then handed it gracefully back to Standing Arrow as if she were passing a china teapot. She smiled, curtsied and said, "Thank you for your gift!"

Everyone laughed—even Standing Arrow.

Elizabeth skinned and quartered the deer while Katie helped her mother fix supper. When the meal was ready, Ellen decided to have some fun. She handed Standing Arrow a jar of pickled eggs.

He studied the eggs floating in the jar, but was unsure what to do with them, so he lifted the jar to his nose, which wrinkled immediately from the pungent smell.

Ellen giggled girlishly. Reaching for the jar, she plucked out an egg and bit into it daintily. Standing Arrow understood the game now. Reaching into the cold liquid, he took out an egg and popped the whole thing into his mouth. The sour taste startled him, causing him to make a funny face. Ellen laughed and continued to eat her egg delicately. Standing Arrow chewed his egg, giving Elizabeth a wink as he swallowed it.

The rest of the meal went smoothly. Standing Arrow had relaxed, and Ellen seemed to enjoy his company. She brought out an apple pie to complete the meal, serving Standing Arrow the first and biggest piece. Although no words were spoken, when their eyes met momentarily Ellen knew Standing Arrow was teasing her and was asking if it was safe to eat this unknown food.

"Go ahead. It's good. You'll like it," laughed Ellen.

After the meal, the small group of travelers gathered around one large fire. Laban squeezed in as close to Standing Arrow as he could get without being rude. Sarah sat by her mother and tried hard not to stare at the tall bronze man. Ellie marched boldly over to Standing Arrow and leaned on his knees while see stared deep into his eyes. The young chief lifted the four-year-old and deposited her on his lap. Smiling, Ellie put her arms around Standing Arrow and hugged him.

Mrs. Larson tried to quietly coax Ellie to come to her, but Ellie wanted no part of it. She was content to stay in the arms of the Cheyenne chief.

Laban, unable to remain quiet, started asking Standing Arrow questions. "Have you killed a bear with your arrows? Are you really a Chief? Can I be a warrior? How much farther to your town?"

Standing Arrow tried to keep up with the questions, but finally gave up, laughing at the young boy. "At Cheyenne village you must learn the ways of my people First lesson, to only ask chief question in Cheyenne language," Standing Arrow said in mock sternness.

Everyone laughed, except Laban. He looked thoughtful for a minute and then announced, "But I don't know how to speak the Cheyenne language. You already speak

English, so maybe it would be easier if you learned how to understand my questions."

The entire group laughed and Standing Arrow replied, "We think about you being a warrior."

The following morning when Standing Arrow rode out of his camp and into the Mayfields' camp, Laban was saddled and waiting. Riding up beside Standing Arrow, Laban ask eagerly, "Can I ride with you?"

With a grin, Standing Arrow nodded and replied, "I go speak to Elizabeth. Then we ride. You can meet my friends."

"Is Elizabeth your girlfriend?" asked Laban curiously.

Unfamiliar with the term "girlfriend" and the white man's ways, Standing Arrow replied, "I will give her father many strong ponies for her!"

This time it was Laban who was confused. "You are going to buy her?" he asked in unbelief.

Standing Arrow thought for a moment before he answered, smiling. "I give her father ponies. He gives me Elizabeth. We trade."

"Trade!" repeated Laban as he shook his head. "I have a lot to learn about wild Indians!"

Standing Arrow laughed and agreed that he too had a lot to learn about the white man's ways.

Elizabeth watched them riding away, wondering if Standing Arrow would be able to endure the boy's constant questioning. Riding into the trees, Standing Arrow led the small boy swiftly, weaving in and out among trees until they joined the warriors. Standing Arrow spoke to the braves in Cheyenne tongue, telling them that the boy wanted to ride with them and be a warrior.

Laban didn't approach the warriors as readily as he did Standing Arrow. Sitting around the campfire with his parents and the Mayfields, Laban thought Standing Arrow seemed as harmless as a fly, but in the wooded area, away from the wagons and surrounded by warriors, Laban's mouth went dry and his heart beat a little faster.

Standing Arrow noticed two things immediately: Laban's eyes were like an owl's, and the boy was very quiet. The first could go unnoticed, but the second one caused Standing Arrow to realize the boy was scared. The chief told Laban the names of each brave. Nakoma and Swift Elk smiled cheerfully at the boy, but the other two merely nodded.

Laban relaxed a little but stayed close beside Standing Arrow all morning. Standing Arrow showed the boy signs and animal tracks along the way. Once they came upon a mother bear and a small cub. Swift Elk pointed them out to Laban, but used sign language to tell him to be quiet and very still. The small group of warriors watched the bears for a few minutes. Then, like the wind, they disappeared over the next ridge leaving the bears unharmed.

Farther down the trail Standing Arrow spoke to Laban. "Bear meat good to eat!"

Forgetting his fear Laban answered quickly. "I've never eaten bear before. When we get to your town can we eat bear?"

"Only very strong warriors hunt bear! Are you strong?" asked Standing Arrow.

Laban thought on this a few minutes and then replied. "I don't think I'm that strong—but you are!"

Standing Arrow chuckled and translated what Laban had said to his braves. Swift Elk smiled broadly and thought to himself that with the right training this small boy would make a good warrior.

When the wagons halted for a quick lunch break, Standing Arrow and Laban left the warriors and made their way through the small ravine that separated them from the wagons.

Laban made up for the silence of the warriors during the noon meal. He told about the bears and about each warrior and how they were dressed in leather with beads and feathers and flat colored strips on the arms and legs. Pausing to take a breath, he finished his recitation by confidently saying, "I'm going to be a brave warrior!"

Everyone laughed, including Standing Arrow.

The next morning Standing Arrow told them they would be coming into the Cheyenne encampment before lunchtime. The excitement among them seemed to spread. Even the mules quickened their steps.

The warriors rode with the wagons now and Laban rode beside Swift Elk. Daniel's wagon was the first in line and therefore he was the first to sight the village.

Stopping the mules, Daniel stood taking in the view. Ellen drew in her breath at the sight of the majestic tepees nestled on the valley floor. The top of each tepee was darkened from the smoke that lazily rolled out of the open flaps. A river wound gracefully along one side of the valley, and trees encased the valley on both sides. Ellen's eyes rested on a woman running toward them. The spell was broken when a warrior rode swiftly past them towards the woman.

Nakoma lifted Yellow Flower effortlessly and she swung up behind him. She was eager to fill him in on the happenings at the village. Yellow Flower quickly told him about the wedding feast and that Rain Song was one of the chosen maidens.

Nakoma was angry, but decided now wasn't the time to tell Standing Arrow—or Swift Elk. He noticed Swift Elk looking around for Rain Song. She always met him when he returned. *This is not a good thing,* thought Nakoma. Something like this would hurt many of the Cheyenne people, and the small group of whites might not want to stay and teach the people.

Chapter Nineteen

The Cheyenne people gathered around the two wagons, anxious and curious to see the white men and their families.

Laban jumped down from his father's wagon and started talking to the Indian boys that looked to be about the same age as he was. They didn't understand him, but felt the friendship and began to talk back to him.

Elizabeth and Katie were absorbed into the crowd immediately by women who wanted hugs.

Standing Arrow stood back and watched. Rain Song boldly approached him and made her desire for marriage known to him. Brushing her aside, he stalked off angrily. *What is she doing?* wondered Standing Arrow. *She is promised to Swift Elk.*

He hadn't gone far when Red Sky approached him and did likewise. This time he was really angry. Standing Arrow had never been known to be rude, but in his anger he turned abruptly and walked away. In short order, he found Yellow Flower. Taking her elbow, he led her away from the crowd and into the privacy of her tepee.

"What is going on?" he demanded.

Yellow Flower dropped her gaze to the ground as tears filled her soft brown eyes. "I tried to stop it. I couldn't think of anything to do," stammered Yellow Flower.

"Stop it? Stop what?" demanded Standing Arrow.

The tepee door opened and Nakoma entered as a sob escaped from Yellow Flower. Nakoma looked stern and Standing Arrow knew he was about to get the answer he'd came after.

"Two of the old ones decided it was not good for the chief to be lonely," began Nakoma. "They have prepared a wedding feast and chosen two maidens. You must now pick one if you wish to remain the chief. The wedding will be tomorrow afternoon."

A hopelessness washed over Standing Arrow, but he spoke the only words he could. "We must find a way!"

The Larsons and the Mayfields were each given a tepee to live in. The teamster said he'd sleep under a wagon until he headed back to Julesburg. And Trent would be Standing Arrow's guest.

The Larsons quickly unloaded the wagon containing books and school supplies into their new home and then helped the Mayfields unload the food supplies. Mrs. Larson was eager to begin her work here and attempted to speak to several children.

The children were also eager to listen, but it wasn't long before both sides realized they must first learn how to communicate. Language lessons would be difficult. Standing Arrow could speak and understand most English words, and Yellow Flower could understand a little.

Mrs. Larson realized it would be up to Elizabeth to help them undertake this difficult task. She decided she would have Elizabeth teach the children a new word each day. And today she would start with the word "God." It was easy for Elizabeth to explain God to the Cheyenne children because all knew about the Great Spirit.

Laban and Ellie found friends immediately, but Sarah hung back waiting and watching.

After dark, the Mayfields, Standing Arrow and Trent met in Nakoma's lodge to discuss the problem about Standing Arrow having to choose a wife. Elizabeth's heart was breaking. She could never ask Standing Arrow to give up his position as chief, but she didn't think she could live without him. She prayed for strength to face the ordeal.

When everyone had run out of ideas, Ellen spoke up. "You say the old ones each present a maiden and then Standing Arrow has to choose one?"

The heads somberly nodded in agreement.

"Well, I'm kind of old," Ellen said hastily, "and Elizabeth is a maiden. I will present her tomorrow in the ceremony and Standing Arrow can choose her!"

All eyes were fixed on Ellen as she spoke. A flame of hope leaped in each eye. Then, like puppets attached with strings, everyone's eyes shifted and rested on Standing Arrow.

A thoughtful look was replaced by an amused smile. "Mother of Elizabeth would do that?" he asked warily. "Yes," spoke Ellen softly. "Yes, I would," she said firmly.

Excitement filled the tepee, and each wanted to help with the preparations. Elizabeth must be dressed in a new dress and adorned for the ceremony.

Nakoma put more wood on the fire to give light while Yellow Flower pulled out three hides she had just tanned, but had not had time to smoke yet. They were a light creamy color soft and supple.

Elizabeth dug out the quill bag she had labored over during the long winter months and had wanted to give to Standing Arrow. But she decided she had better wear it instead to add more to her costume. She could give it to him later. He would understand.

Yellow Flower surprised her by presenting a wide quill strip for her to put across the front of her dress. With the new scissors and needles that Elizabeth had brought, the four women put together an elaborate dress and moccasins adorned with porcupine quill strips, feathers and beads. Elizabeth borrowed a belt from Yellow Flower, and her outfit was completed with the medallion given to her by Standing Arrow.

Standing Arrow, Nakoma, Trent and Daniel made their way to Standing Arrow's lodge to help him prepare for the wedding. Neither group got much sleep that night. When the village crier made his rounds, it didn't wake either lodge.

Day was shooting crimson arrows into the vast bowl of the sky when Elizabeth awoke. Emerging from the tepee, she drank in the morning air before she stepped onto the path that led to the stream.

Standing Arrow was sitting beside the stream with his back to her. Elizabeth stopped momentarily and Standing Arrow spoke to her. "You will have to learn to step quietly again!"

Elizabeth smiled. "You will have to teach me."

Sitting next to each other, they watched dawn turn to daylight.

The feast had begun and the old women brought out the maidens one at a time and had them stop in front of Standing Arrow. Red Sky was first. She was brought to his right side and left to stand quietly while Rain Song was presented.

Standing Arrow caught sight of Swift Elk stalking off angrily while Rain Song was being presented on his left side. He felt for the young dog soldier that had been betrayed. He would feel the same, he was sure.

Before the two old women could proceed with the ceremony, Ellen came with Elizabeth and boldly presented her to Standing Arrow. She placed Elizabeth right in the middle of the two maidens and directly in front of Standing Arrow. A smile played at the chief's lips but he disciplined it immediately.

Rain Song was the only one who seemed to mind that a third maiden had been added. She had been sure Standing Arrow would choose her over Red Sky. That had been her reason for betraying Swift Elk. She knew Swift Elk was the next best, but she had been sure she would get the chief.

Seeing Standing Arrow's quill medallion around Elizabeth's neck was all the reason she needed to know she had lost both Swift Elk and Standing Arrow. She would have to endure a long ceremony intended to give the chief plenty of time to decide on one maiden, but Rain Song knew that Standing Arrow's mind was already made up.

Holding to a thread of desperation, Rain Song danced wildly in front of the young chief, hoping to change his mind. Red Sky and Elizabeth were both serene and confident. Red Sky knew it was an honor just to be chosen to dance for the chief, and she was not promised to another warrior, so she held her head high and was proud.

Elizabeth knew the chief would pick her, so she was only going through the formalities. Rain Song knew she would be disgraced and should leave the camp at once. Her mind raced while she danced wildly. What should she do?

When the drums quit beating and the dancing stopped, Standing Arrow was to rise and take a maiden by the hand and lead her to his lodge. She would then be his wife. Walking slowly in front of the three maidens, Standing Arrow looked at each, pausing momentarily, playing the part. He turned and made another trip down the line.

Stopping, he reached out and took Elizabeth's hand. The drums beat loudly now and the dancing resumed.

Only this time the whole tribe was dancing. The feast would most likely continue long into the night.

Red Sky blended happily with the crowd, while Rain Song ran shamefully to the edge of the encampment to get away from the crowd. When she reached the trees she kept going at a fast pace. Blind furry moved her farther and farther from camp.

When Standing Arrow and Elizabeth had made their way through the crowd, Standing Arrow scooped Elizabeth up and at the same time he let out a long loud eagle call. He then carried her into his lodge.

"My Dove has returned," he said in Cheyenne.

Smiling, Elizabeth replied in Cheyenne. "I never really left."

THE END

To order additional copies of

CAPTIVE
HEARTS

Listen for the Call

Have your credit card ready and call:

1-877-421-READ (7323)

or please visit our web site at
www.pleasantword.com

Also available at: www.amazon.com

Printed in the United States
1197900002B/67-285